The Return

James
Terry

The Shortish Project | San Francisco
theshortishproject.com

Published 2023 by The Shortish Project

Terry, James
The Return / James Terry
ISBN 9798987839881

Available in print and ebook editions

The Shortish Project is dedicated to expanding
access to short novels, a program welcoming all
styles and genres. For more information and titles,
visit theshortishproject.com.

the
short
ish
project

The
Return

La liberté, c'est le droit au silence.
Freedom is the right to silence.
— Graffiti, Paris, May '68

Professor Aoust reached the theater twenty minutes early, as was his custom, and proceeded down the lefthand aisle to his habitual seat, four rows from the bottom, far left, which through wholly unconscious trial and error he had settled on at some point in the previous decade. This location made it easy to get up and leave should the need arise, not that it often did, but one needed to reserve the right to walk out in disgust on a film without one's escape being encumbered by unobliging knees and feet and bags. Taking his seat, he crossed his legs, the left draped leisurely over the right, the upper foot bobbing every now and then to no discernible rhythm, and pulled yesterday's *Daily Cal* (Tuesday, February 19, 2008) from his case.

There was no place in the world where Bernard Aoust felt happier than alone in a cinema awaiting the start of a film: the virginal white expanse of the screen, the reverential hush of the patrons trickling in in ones and twos, the aura of expectation. And although he didn't mind a little light music as he read his newspaper, a string quartet or classic jazz, in general he scorned film scores themselves as background music, for the imposition of the filmic world onto the real one seemed to him somehow sacrilegious. No matter the stresses of the day or the crises in his life, a sense of calm always befell Aoust in these special few minutes before the start of a film. Emanating from the back of his neck, the calm gradually spread to the rest of his body, never failing to bring a smile to his face, if only in the metaphorical sense, for the casual observer would have been hard-pressed at this moment to see any change at all in the professor's expression behind the thicket of gray and white hairs of his beard and mustache, nicotine-stained in two stripes beneath his nose. But for those trained to see such things there was a most definite relaxation of his muscles and nerves, a sinking of his shoulders, a profound exhalation which ensconced him deeper into the upholstery of his seat, his left trouser leg riding millimeter by millimeter higher to reveal a sagging beige sock and the bluish-white skin of his shin as his torso slid another degree closer to the horizontal, all this sinking and settling culminating in an effortless little flick to his newspaper, a twitch of the wrists as delicate yet deliberate as a percussionist's final ping on the triangle.

Aoust was the author of *The Encyclopedia of French Silent Cinema* (1973), among other, lesser known works, and it was in this capacity that Marsha Cohen, the director of programming at the Pacific Film Archive, had asked him to make a few introductory remarks before tonight's screening of Jules Rodier's *Le Fils prodigue* (1926). Pondering in his idle moments over the past few days what he might say about this handsome but sentimental and not particularly important film, Aoust considered speaking more generally about the parallels between cinema and religious experience, for the feelings he always got in a cinema were, to his mind, the same feelings a religious person experienced in his or her place of worship. He had arrived at this realization many years ago and realized it again every now and then, always with the conviction that it was a novel concept and would make for an interesting paper. He was perfectly aware of the vast body of scholarship on religion and cinema, but those studies tended to focus on the content of a given film, not the feelings of the viewer watching it, which were not the same thing at all, for if they were then one could get the same experience playing a movie at home or, heaven forbid, on one's cell phone. Aoust was more interested in the rituals of worship itself, the sacred space, the recurring congregation of fellow devotees, the state of receptive silence. While professing to be an atheist and believing wholeheartedly in the absolute non-existence of anything remotely supernatural anywhere in the universe, that is to say if push came to shove he would take his stand amongst the empiricists, he could not deny that his devotion to cinema was much more than an intellectual pursuit.

Before the start of the film, Marsha took to the podium and welcomed the audience to this the second program in the weeklong series of French silent films from the 1920s, the prelude to the season of films commemorating the 40th anniversary of the events of May '68 in France. She then introduced Professor Aoust with a flattering synopsis of his career, emphasizing his passion for silent cinema, at which point he made his way to the microphone and, clearing an inopportune clump of phlegm from his throat, thanked her for her kind remarks. Not as briefly as promised, Aoust spoke about the history of Rodier's film, the genre it belonged to, the director's biography and filmography, etc., but the most important thing he wanted to impart to tonight's audience was that *Le Fils prodigue* was the inferior younger cousin of Michel Defoix's astonishing film, *Le Retour* (1923). Whereas *Le Fils prodigue* told the prodigal son story in conventional form, *Le Retour*, the lost film, broke nearly every convention of the time— moral, aesthetic, political and otherwise. If the members of the audience had never heard of *Le Retour*, or of Michel Defoix for that matter, it was because *Le Retour* was the only film that Michel Defoix had ever made, and, as far as Aoust knew, the last surviving print had perished during the Occupation. The film began to surface again, in phantom form, in Paris after the war, in the memories of people who had seen it, but now they themselves were nothing but memories. In fact it would not be an exaggeration to say that the only place where Michel Defoix's *Le Retour* could be seen anymore in anything resembling its entirety was in the mind of Bernard Aoust. Not that he himself had ever seen the complete film. The last (and only) known public screening was on Friday, November 23, 1923, at the Vieux-Colombier in Paris, a quarter of a century before Aoust was born. All that remained of the film was 681 feet of time-ravaged celluloid in the vaults of the Cinémathèque Française. Every now and then Aoust would come across a passing reference to *Le Retour* in a film journal or edited volume, always with the addendum "(no print survives)," which, even now, nearly four decades after he had first read that terrible phrase, still struck him as unbearably tragic. In a just world it was *Le Fils prodigue*, the film they were about to watch, that should have been forgotten.

"But," he said in closing, "time has a way of lending a certain charm to even the unexceptional cultural artifacts of the past, and I don't wish to take away from the simple pleasures of *Le Fils prodigue* and so will say no more."

A smattering of applause, and Aoust returned to his seat. While he was speaking, a woman had taken the seat beside his, which he'd been hoping would remain empty. A quick glance revealed middle-age, stoutness, shortish blondish hair. The strong, musky scent of her perfume provided a more lasting impression. Just before the lights went down she leaned over and said in a playful whisper:

"Say something in French."

"Pardon?" Aoust replied, tilting his head a little her way.

She repeated it.

She couldn't possibly be serious. It was something a child or a complete ignoramus would say. Maybe she was being ironic, he thought, subtly mocking the kind of woman who would say such a thing to a man she didn't even know, in which case he owed her a little chuckle at the very least. She waited, all eagerness. No, he concluded. She was just stupid. But if she really was that stupid, what was she doing at the PFA? Granted, even stupid people sometimes ended up in places they didn't belong.

"Le garçon déroula la carte," he said, simply to be done with it.

She smiled, and though it wasn't exactly detectable to the naked eye, he sensed a shiver roll through her.

At last the lights dimmed, and Aoust sank once more into the depths of his seat. He was briefly agitated by the dirt and scratches marring the opening credits of a supposedly new 35mm print, but a few shots into the first reel it cleared up, and he gave himself over to the charming, melancholy world of *Le Fils prodigue* and forgot all about the irritating woman, who apart from a few snuffling noises during the film had ceased entirely to exist.

Aoust stayed seated through the entirety of the closing credits, as was also his custom, even as the lights came up to allow those who wished to leave the theater to do so. He kept expecting the woman, who had suddenly rematerialized, to get up and excuse herself as she tried to squeeze past his knees. But she didn't. She too remained rooted to her seat until the film hit the leader with a satisfying pop, the screen blazed white, and the projectionist closed the dowser. Not only was the woman still there, but Aoust could see in his peripheral vision that she was gazing in rapturous silence at the blank screen, a trail of tears glistening on her nearest cheek. Seeing as they were the only people left in the theater, Aoust felt that it would be rather rude of him to just get up and walk out without some kind of acknowledgement of her presence. He turned and gave her a strained smile. She reached into her bag and pulled out a tissue and dabbed at her cheeks. At last they stood up, and as they headed slowly up the aisle, Aoust realized that she wasn't merely behind him; she was *with* him, and he was escorting her out.

His retinas still intoxicated by the dense blacks and soft whites of the film, it took his eyes a moment to readjust to the contours and colors of reality. Across from the theater, Hearst Gymnasium's monumental concrete walls loomed up into the night sky like the Parthenon, its terraces and balustrades giving way to cornices and pediments. A solitary streetlamp shed a warm peach-colored glow beneath the dark, leafless canopy of the live oak and camphor laurels sheltering the theater from the street. The final ritual of a satisfying cinema experience, and perhaps the one Aoust loved most, was walking home under the spell of a fine film, smoking a cigarette, taking his time, observing everything around him as if through the lens of a motion picture camera, especially after a silent film, even one with a superfluous piano score, when every sound that greeted his ears — footsteps, car horns, laughter, music — seemed newly minted.

Desperate for a cigarette, Aoust reached into his bag and pulled out the pack.

"I'll join you," the woman said, reaching into her purse.

Aoust lit hers first, and they stood together for a moment, gazing at nothing in particular.

"So I take it you like silent films?" he asked her after they had each taken a drag.

"I guess I do," she replied as if it were a

revelation even to her.

Side by side they descended the stairs to Bancroft Way.

"I always thought they were kind of hokey," she admitted as they reached the sidewalk, "something stagey about them. But this was different. It was magical."

Aoust nodded. He actually preferred this kind of naive appreciation to the arrogance of his students, who were no doubt already ripping the film apart, eager to validate their favorite theories, those who had bothered to come at all. As a teacher his main hope was that his students would take away from his classes something of his love of silent cinema, but nowadays it seemed they were all too sophisticated and theoretical and militant and drenched in identity politics and bent on progressing their causes and finding racism and misogyny and bigotry and various other evils lurking in everything they viewed.

"This staginess you speak of," he said, looking somewhere to the right of her head. "There is strange power in this. The gesture. The absence of speech. As if they are aware of us watching them from behind a soundproof glass. In their desire to communicate with us they exaggerate their emotions. And so we have what appears to our modern eyes to be theatrical gestures. They open their mouths as if to speak, but nothing emerges, and yet they themselves aren't aware of their impairment. They behave as if they can hear one another. Because in their world they do in fact hear one another. They are reacting to sounds that we ourselves cannot hear.

It is *we* who are impaired, not them."

Only now did Aoust look at her, and he saw on her face a look of enchantment—the effect of his words or his accent, he couldn't say. Perhaps his initial assessment of her hadn't been so charitable. On an impulse, he asked her if she would care to join him for a cup of coffee.

"That would be nice," she said. Her name was Margaret, by the way.

Crossing the street at the next opportunity, Aoust led Margaret up the block to Caffè Strada, where the rich aroma of superlative dark Arabicas assailed them from the sidewalk. They made their way in through the illuminated courtyard busy with students staring into their laptops, and as they waited to be served she admired all the wonderful cakes and pies and fruit tarts beckoning from their glass display cases. Aoust intuited from her expressions of delight at the café's European charms that Berkeley was not her native domain, that she had ventured into civilization from Outer Barbaria.

She ordered a piece of lemon meringue pie and a glass of hazelnut Italian soda. He ordered an espresso and paid for hers as well.

"Can we sit outside?" she requested. "It's such a lovely night."

They found a table beneath the pear trees on the College Avenue side.

She started right in with the questions. How long had he been in America? Did he miss France? How had he become a professor of cinema? He answered in a perfunctory way, preferring to talk about films, not himself.

"And you?" he asked.

She pulled a card from her purse and handed it to him. *Margaret Perkins. Real Estate Broker.*

"Need a house?" she joked, laughing vigorously.

She then asked Aoust about that other film he had mentioned — she couldn't remember the title — and he described for her some of the salient features of *Le Retour*: its unique visualization of consumer culture, so far ahead of its time; the lingering shots of mass-produced products in shop windows, hand-tinted red to reveal their deeper function as objects of sensual desire; how in its flow of images, in the sequences of alternating shots between glossy consumer goods and images of poverty, the film pits the powerful against the powerless: ragged men standing in line for a bowl of soup while a proper young gentleman in an elegant restaurant polishes off a beefsteak, mansions and shopping arcades juxtaposed with garbage dumps, smoky tenements, desolate alleys, crumbling concrete; how the film subverts the prodigal son story to present a scathing critique of capitalism, of the family, the Church, bourgeois society, of cinema itself, doing so, Aoust explained, with cinematographic techniques so avant-garde that much of the film was barely comprehensible to the audience of its day.

"Perhaps the most radical innovation," Aoust informed her with growing enthusiasm as she polished off her lemon meringue, "the intentional scratching of the surface of the film, which was undreamed of in even the most avant-garde cinema circles of the day, came about in relation to the other revolutionary, and by far the most shocking, feature of *Le Retour*: the pornographic sex scene." Margaret's eyes widened appropriately. "When Defoix screened the first edit of his film, which purportedly ran to a length of 111 minutes, to Jacques Copeau, the proprietor of the Vieux-Colombier, Copeau, aghast, replied that it was absolutely impossible to show this film in his theater. It would never get past the censors. Copeau told him to edit out the sex scene and drastically cut the film—only then would he even begin to entertain the possibility of screening it. But rather than cut the sex scene, Defoix chose to thumb his finger at the censors by manually scratching out the offending body parts from every frame with a dental instrument. Copeau surely would not have allowed even this in his theater, but as luck would have it, in the fall of 1923, Jean Tedesco, an influential critic and filmmaker, took over as the managing director of the Vieux-Colombier, with the intention of screening avant-garde films. It was to Jean Tedesco that Defoix showed his altered print. The rest, as they say, is film history."

"Wow," she said. "I'd love to see it."

"Why not?" Aoust replied. "Come, I'll show it to you."

"Right now?" she asked, looking somewhat confused.

"Yes, why not? What remains of it, at least."

"Where?"

"My house. I have a videotape. Where are you parked?"

She smiled with bemusement for a few more seconds then told him.

"Come," he said, scooting his chair back and standing up. "My apartment is on the way."

Then, adopting a spirit of harmless adventure, she stood up and said, "Okay."

Aoust's building was on Dwight Way, between Dana and Elsworth, three blocks over and four blocks down from the café, passing People's Park along the way. Tonight the five-minute walk seemed longer than usual, as Margaret, apparently more nervous than she was letting on, delivered an extended monologue on the current state of the housing market.

Reaching the building, Aoust keyed in his code and led her up the stairs to the second floor, apologizing for the mess as he unlocked the door and showed her in, though in truth he felt no shame about the state of his living space. During the twenty-one years of his marriage, he had managed more or less to rein in his slovenly nature and do his part to keep at least the communal spaces of their house tidy, but after the divorce and his demotion to this one-bedroom rental on the south side of campus, his true instincts returned, and like unchecked nature recolonizing an abandoned industrial site, the detritus of his daily life was allowed to accumulate wherever it pleased: stacks of books, journals, magazines, newspapers, CDs, DVDs, cigarette cartons, coffee cups, ashtrays, and, most of all, great precarious towers of VHS videotapes, all of it saturated with the stale odor of a decade's worth of cigarette smoke.

"Wow, look at all these videotapes!" Margaret exclaimed. "You really are old school."

"Can I get you something to drink? I have port, vermouth, absinthe, Diet Coke."

She chose the port, and he went into the kitchen and poured her a glass. When he returned to the living room she was kneeling in the corner, petting the cat where she lay on one of the sofa's reappropriated seat cushions.

"What's his name?"

"Her. Musidora."

"Musidora," she sweetly repeated. "Lovely name."

"Black and white, naturally," Aoust dryly observed, but evidently she didn't get the joke. "Great French actress of the silent era."

It took him a while to find the tape. As a rule he tried to keep his silent stuff in the stacks against the wall to the right of the kitchen doorway, but while searching there for a particular handwritten spine label with light-blue trim, he vaguely recalled having seen it sometime in the recent past somewhere where it didn't belong, though he couldn't presently remember where, so he started to look in a more random fashion, grabbing substacks and moving them out of the way, checking the piles set aside on shelves and other resting places for specific purposes no longer relevant. In his quest, he knocked a dead plant off of a bookshelf, or more precisely a plastic pot with rockhard soil in it and a gray wisp of something that may once have aspired to planthood. Bending down to pick it up, he noticed a promising pile of stuff on the lower tier of the coffee table. There, hidden beneath the drooping pages of the first draft of an article for *Early Popular Visual Culture* that he had started and subsequently abandoned a year and a half ago, he found the videotape.

Wheeling the TV cart closer to the sofa, he powered everything up, put the tape in, grabbed the remotes from the coffee table, and took a seat directly beside Margaret on one of the two remaining sofa cushions and hit play.

"Feel free to smoke," he said, but she politely declined the offer, and so, although desperate for another cigarette, he, too, refrained.

The film begins, if not at its true beginning, with a young man (Michel Defoix himself) in extreme close-up, this shot answered a few moments later by a close-up of a cow's face, then back and forth in quick succession between cow and man gazing into each other's eyes as if contemplating some profound question, the sequence culminating in a shot of the cow lying dead in a pool of blood. Then, with shocking suddenness, the dead cow leaps up from the ground, back to a standing position, its blood funneling against the laws of gravity back into its severed neck, the butcher's long blade sealing the gash and reversing the flow of blood.

Aoust could sense in the tenor of her silence that Margaret did not like what she was seeing and was perhaps now questioning the wisdom of her decision to enter the apartment of a man she knew nothing about, and he also sensed, in the subsequent change in her breathing, her relief as the scene shifted to Michel and his father and brother eating dinner in the lantern-lit darkness of the humble farmhouse. It had been a while since Aoust had watched the film in the presence of another human being, and it was gratifying to hear Margaret chortle when the horse walks backwards down Rue Pastourelle, to hear her gasp when Nadia, instead of a fish, rises from the Seine on the end of Michel's fishing line. Margaret's reactions lent some freshness to the film, so that when it abruptly ended with Nadia in mid-stride, walking not to the door of Michel's squalid garret but into oblivion, Aoust felt a sharper than usual pang of loss. With every passing year this sensation of irreparable loss only seemed to increase, leaving him feeling every time he watched these sole surviving scraps like the first time his heart was broken, because for Aoust the story of *Le Retour* had long since ceased to be the story as told within the film, the story lost with the loss of the prints, and had become instead the story *of* that loss, surpassing by many magnitudes of complexity and emotion anything that Michel Defoix could ever have created, encompassing such disparate subjects as the economic and political climate of Europe in 1923, the flourishing of new tendencies in art in the interwar period, the powerful experimental tradition of the early French film pioneers, Michel Defoix's and Nadia Marinescu's biographies, the looming threat of sound, the biblical parable of the prodigal son, France's early pornographic film industry, Marxism and the rise of the consumer class, the film journals of the period, Paris's cine clubs, not to mention all the intense emotions Aoust associated with that magical time in his

life when at last he had found his true calling —
that was the story that began with the close-up of
Michel Defoix's eyes and ended abruptly seven
minutes and thirty-four seconds later with Nadia
Marinescu vanishing mid-stride — every scratch,
every speck of dust playing a role in Aoust's own
private *Le Retour*.

Aoust pressed stop on the remote and turned
to observe his guest.

"That's it?" she said, looking baffled.

Aoust solemnly nodded. "All that's left of it,
I'm afraid."

"No sex scene?"

"No sex scene."

"Hmm. Well. Very interesting. I can't say
I understood all of it, but, yeah, I see what you
mean."

Aoust stood up, cleared the phlegm from his
mildly aching throat, and rolled the TV cart back
to its spot.

"Well, I guess I should be shoving off,"
Margaret said, standing up. "Thank you so much
for a most charming evening."

Aoust nodded, knowing it would be futile to
try to explain to her all that she was missing, and
showed her to the door.

"I'll walk you down."

"Oh no, I'm a big girl. I can find my way
out."

Aoust leaned forward to give her the three
kisses to her cheeks that were her due, but
apparently thinking he was aiming for her lips
she met him halfway with hers and kissed him,
softly at first and then with more passion.

"Would you like me to stay?" she asked quietly.

"Oui," he said.

•

There were many aspects of Telegraph Avenue that annoyed Aoust — the aging hippies, the morose or cheery homeless men and their sleeping dogs, the tourists obliviously clogging the sidewalks, the smell of incense, the strung-out teenagers begging for money and seeming to think it was cool, the ubiquitous tie-dye T-shirts, the New Age jewelry, the rivers of students with their bulging backpacks — but he still cherished after all these years the feeling of vibrant city life that a few-block stroll down Telegraph gave him. On a pleasantly cool and sunny late winter day such as this he could almost forget all the misery in the world.

Approaching the south side of campus, Aoust heard a voice on a loudspeaker making an impassioned speech, the words of which he couldn't make out at this distance. It was coming from Sproul Plaza, one of the usual noon rallies for some hopeless cause or other. At the corner of Bancroft and Telegraph, Aoust stopped and waited with a clutch of students for the traffic light to change as the cars flowed by in a continuous downhill stream. Two burly campus cops on the other side of the street stood with arms crossed at their chests, talking to each other. The light changed, and Aoust crossed the street with the horde.

Proceeding through Sproul Plaza's colonnade of London plane trees, whose pollarded branches, bulging at the joints like arthritic knuckles, were still bare, Aoust could now make out fairly clearly every fifth or sixth word of the speaker, as well as the answering approval of the crowd, a sound that no matter the merits of the cause never failed to fill him with anxiety, which he not unreasonably traced back to his father's stories of the Nazis, compounded by subsequent viewings of *Triumph of the Will* and the rest of Riefenstahl's ouvre. Not fond of communal fervor in any shape or form, Aoust veered around the back of the crowd, which he estimated at several hundred students. Venturing a quick glance above their heads — he halted his progress to confirm it — he saw that the person speaking was one of his students, the guy in the Tuesday-Thursday afternoon section of History of Film 1 with the long greasy hair who always wore a black leather jacket and sat at the back with his earbuds in his ears, radiating smug indifference. Aoust couldn't at that moment recall his name, but standing up there behind the microphone, turning side to side to take in the entirety of his audience, pausing to measure the effect of his words, this kid who rarely uttered a word in class was transformed.

Aoust stopped and listened.

"...a serious look at ourselves and ask what we can do to stop this madness, or we're finished. They say the politicians are working on it. Well, I'm sorry, they're not working on it. The politicians have all been bought off. The scientists are working on it; they'll figure it out, they always do. Yeah, right. This unquestioned belief in science and technology to solve everything is the whole problem."

Aoust stood for a few more moments, listening without being able to discern what exactly the student was advocating, if anything, then, glancing up at the campanile and seeing that it was five past one, he hurried on through Sather Gate and into Dwinelle Hall.

Sprawled across a broad slope declining to the north and west, Dwinelle had seven entrances at four different altitudes and was internally divided into two wings, the north and the south, whose schizophrenic layout gave birth to the myth that the building had been created by two feuding brothers. The north wing consisted of seven stories of departmental and faculty offices, whereas the south wing, which housed the classrooms, had only five, not counting the basement; none of which explained why the floors of the north wing were four feet lower than their counterparts in the south wing, necessitating steps for the able bodied and ramps for the physically challenged to cross the otherwise invisible threshold from north to south and vice versa. Perhaps in an effort to formalize and make more apparent the divisions within the building, but which in fact only made things more confusing, the room numbers in the south wing bore no relationship whatsoever to the room numbers in the north wing, resulting in the peculiar situation that room number 324 on level F of the south wing shared part of a wall with office number 6218 on the same level of the north wing. Even people who had worked in the building for decades, if forced by an out-of-order elevator or a stairwell getting a fresh coat of paint to take an alternative route, could find themselves as disoriented as a sleepwalker abruptly awoken in somebody else's house.

Entering through the main doors of the south wing, Aoust made his way through the throngs of students to the elevator and up to level D, where he was surprised to see when he reached the classroom that it was empty. Not a single student in any of the chairs. Even the lights were off. He looked at his watch. A quarter after one (meaning ten after). He stood in the doorway trying to fathom the cause of this. His first thought was that somehow he had gotten the day wrong, but upon further reflection he ruled that out, absolutely certain that it was Tuesday, since yesterday was Monday; he was sure of that because the doctor's appointment that he had bailed on had been yesterday.

He looked again at his watch. "Must be some...," he mumbled. "Give them another ten..."

Turning on the lights, he set his case on the table and pulled out his folder and the reader and took a seat. Soon the rest of the building settled into the relative quiet of the teaching hour. Through the stillness Aoust could still faintly hear the voice of the student over the loudspeaker. Only then did it dawn on him that this student, for one, would not be attending class today, and he wondered if the rally had anything to do with the absence of the others, though he found it highly unlikely that every one of his students would have skipped class to listen to this individual. No doubt there was a simple explanation, which would soon be revealed to him, some announcement he hadn't received from the department secretary, though he had to acknowledge the unsettling possibility that every one of his students, acting individually, or perhaps collectively, had decided to quit his class on the same day—that there was truth after all to Schroft's allegations that he was the least popular professor in the Film department. Under the circumstances, it was hard not to feel that somehow the empty classroom was part of her conspiracy to get rid of him. A few weeks after her appointment last fall as the new chair of the department, Andrea Schroft had called Aoust to her office for a private meeting and offered him an early retirement deal, wherein if he were to make this his final year of teaching he would receive his full pension plus a very attractive severance package. And when he asked her why she felt compelled to send him into early retirement — he was only sixty, after all, and he knew plenty of professors who worked well into their seventies — she was diplomatic, presenting it as a matter of budgetary considerations, the numbers of film majors having fallen for three consecutive years, and she was being "forced by higher powers" to find places to make cuts, but he suspected that the real reason he was being targeted was that she and other members of the department, particularly Charles Nashe, the other French film scholar (who wasn't even French but Canadian), were seeking to push the department in a new direction, clear the "dead wood" from the ranks, bring in new, young (cheaper) faculty.

Of course she didn't say it outright, that she felt Aoust's work was no longer of any interest to the students of today, but she as much as implied it when she said that kids these days found it hard to sit through silent films, much less write dissertations about them. Her gambit to buy him off not succeeding, it fell to Schroft's allies in the department to try to make Aoust's professional life as miserable as possible, going through elaborate contortions to avoid acknowledging his existence in any way on the rare occasions when they were in the same general vicinity, not including him in any departmental activities, not seeking his opinions on curricular matters, never inviting him to be on hiring committees, etc.—which was ironic, for he felt that, having recovered from the sting of Schroft's admonishments, he was actually making progress and was now willing to admit that there was room for improvement, especially in his teaching style, even if he firmly disagreed with her assessment of his scholarship, which, while perhaps not as voluminous as some of his colleagues', represented a lasting contribution to the field. Moreover, he was confident that he had finally turned a corner on the Defoix book. Watching *Le Retour* again the other night with the real estate broker had released something in him—he was reluctant to say inspired him, but practically the first thing he did the next morning was pull out that old shoebox full of microcassettes with a burning to desire to hear Defoix's voice again. And if he was thwarted in that endeavor by what at first he thought were dead batteries but in the end proved to be the expiration of the machine itself, what mattered was that he felt, and more importantly continued to feel nearly a week later, a renewed desire to start writing.

All of which made the empty classroom feel like an unfair judgement against him, because despite what anyone said about him he still found some gratification in his interactions with the students—not all of them, mind you, but certainly the intelligent ones, the ones who showed a genuine interest in what he was trying to impart to them. Their youth, their unsullied hope, their charming naïvete, their unquestioning faith in the American dream, even their wretched diet of Hollywood movies stimulated him on the rare occasion when one of them would come to see him during office hours, absolving him a little of his guilt for not being the best lecturer. But sometimes an unhappy student would come to him, some brazen kid who had no qualms about speaking his or her mind, and would complain to his face about everything that was wrong with his class, that he gave them all this reading and made no effort to clarify or elaborate on any of these dense texts that seemed to have nothing at all to do with cinema, and the manner in which he shut down any kind of free and spontaneous dialogue in the class. Yes, there were some rude students out there these days, imbued with the notion that they were paying customers and weren't happy with the service they had purchased and they were making their dissatisfaction known to the management and expected some redress.

Aoust looked up from his lecture notes, and under the circumstances they did seem a little wanting. This was the same lecture on the grammar of silent cinema that he'd been giving for the past twenty years. Every now and then he might incorporate some new piece of information, an off-the-cuff anecdote if he was in the mood, or a reference to some emerging theory, if only to casually dismiss it as groundless gibberish.

The voice of the student had ceased, and all that could be heard as Aoust continued to sit in the empty classroom were the muted voices of other lecturers, the occasional chair scooting across the floor above, birds chirping somewhere outside the windows. When by 1:30 no one had shown, he decided there was no point sitting there wasting his time any longer, so he returned his lecture notes and the reader to his case, got up, switched off the lights and headed back down the hall to the elevator, dreading all the while that he would run into one of his students making his or her way breathlessly down the hall armed with apologies and excuses, for now that he was free he realized that this was actually a pleasant turn of events, a little gift of unexpected time to do with as he pleased. Not that he had anything particular in mind; but that, after all, was precisely the beauty of it.

Leaving the building, intent on avoiding any of his students who might be hanging around out front, Aoust cut across to the pathway leading around the south side of Dwinelle, down into the chilly shade of the redwoods, across Strawberry Creek via the stepping stones, then up the opposite bank and into Lower Sproul Plaza. Breathing easier now, he skirted Zellerbach Hall and crossed Bancroft at Dana, proceeding from there to Dwight Way and home.

There was a message waiting for him on his answering machine.

"Hi, Professor Aoust. It's Sheryl." — the Film department secretary — "Several of your students from your one o'clock came by the office asking if there'd been a change of schedule. I wasn't aware of any. I hope you're well. Please give me a call when you get this."

He played it again. He picked up the phone and dialed.

"I was there at one."

"That's strange. Three of your students came in asking if you were sick. Are you sure you were in the right room?"

"Of course I'm sure. 324. There was obviously some kind of mix-up. I don't know about the students who came to you, but there was a rally in Sproul Plaza. One of my students was speaking. I'm sure that had something to do with it."

"Oh well. These things happen. I'm glad you're feeling okay."

Aoust hung up the phone, shooing away this nonsense as if it were a pesky fly.

•

Saturday morning, after his coffees and his first half pack of cigarettes and a breakfast of unbuttered toast and milky oatmeal, Aoust walked down to Shattuck Avenue and took BART one stop to Ashby station and there got out to behold, as he did every now and then when he needed something that he knew would be difficult to find anyplace else, the entire two-acre parking lot given over to the vendors of the Berkeley Flea Market, a small inland sea of used clothes, books, vintage postcards, tools, furniture, "art," sunglasses, kitchen utensils, old cameras, cell phone accessories, cleaning supplies, soaps and body oils, handmade jewelry, food stalls, and much much more, all animated by African drumming and the general good vibes of the broad sampling of humanity on display. Even when he had nothing particular in mind, Aoust always found something he couldn't resist buying, like his current VCR, which he had bought for five dollars from the guy who sold old VHS tapes for fifty cents a piece—mostly Hollywood crap but now and then one could find a rare gem buried in the piles.

In Aoust's pocket was a microcassette, brought along to test the device should he be lucky enough to find one, which eventually he did at the stall of a portly, middle-aged Black man wearing an Oakland A's ballcap, sitting in full sunlight on a folding metal chair surrounded by boxes of AC adaptors, cables, reel-to-reel tape recorders, eight-track decks, microphones, speakers, boomboxes, and other obsolete audio gear. As Aoust made his inquiry, the man hauled out from the bottom of a cardboard box three different microcassette player/recorders, and putting fresh batteries in one of them, he inserted the cassette ("Emile Rostan 07-09-72 – Paris") and hit play, and to Aoust's delight the tiny gears began to turn. Holding the speaker to his ear,

Aoust heard again the reedy voice of an old man, barely audible above the din of drumming, but still, he could make out the words, and that was all that mattered.

Back in his apartment Aoust brewed a fresh cafetière and brought the shoebox of tapes over to the folding card table on which he ate his meals and sometimes ironed his shirts. Clearing away the breakfast things, he lit a cigarette, pulled the ashtray closer, pressed play on the machine, and listened to this man named Emile Rostan, whom he could no longer remember, saying in a halting manner something, it seemed, about a milk wagon and a dog. It was difficult for Aoust to separate the man's voice from all the street noise in the background, recorded, by the sound of it, at one of the sidewalk tables of either the Dôme or Daguerre, the only two cafés at which Aoust could recall doing his recordings for the Paris sessions. It took his ears some time to adjust to the lax enunciation and strong accent of this fellow, which after a run of Languedocien vowels he eventually placed as Marseillais, after which the man's visage suddenly snapped into focus (lean, sun-leathered face with a sharp line of contrast high on his forehead courtesy of his years of dedicated service to the French postal service), bringing back with it a whole ensemble of associations: the man's thin and fraying blue coat, the way he had of twisting around nervously in his chair, the pride with which he had spoken of his former route in the 13th — Aoust remembered this detail because the man had made much of passing the former home of Georges Duhamel every day — but he couldn't determine precisely what the man was talking about, for it didn't seem to have anything to do with *Le Retour*, but rather was something about a neighbor and a traffic fine and a Monsieur Bonnay's dog. Aoust pressed the fast forward button for a few seconds, which on this machine didn't disengage the playback heads but simply sped up the tape, amplifying the sound to a painful screel. He did this multiple times, until it became apparent that this was just blather after the meat of the interview, so he stopped the machine, rewound the tape back to the beginning, and started to listen again.

It was then that he heard his own voice — he almost didn't recognize it — and was stunned by the sudden collapse of thirty-six years, the toll that four decades of smoking had taken on his lungs and vocal cords. He sounded so young! Not only physically, but intellectually. He could forgive himself the arrogance of youth, his ambition, his ego, plain to hear in the tone of his questions, for these things were natural and healthy in a man of twenty-four; it was the distinct note of falsity he heard that pained him now, the unwarranted exuberance that he had always identified as a distinctly American trait, clearly already there in him long before he ever set foot in America, for like every French youth of his generation he had been fascinated by America, the America of the movies, the gangsters, the cowboys, Elvis Presley. He had dreamed since childhood of coming to America, certainly not for the rest of his life but maybe for a year or two, and hearing now this excess of enthusiasm in his voice, which he must have unconsciously imbibed from American movies and music, it was painfully clear, more than he had ever suspected at the time, that he was destined to end up here, forever a frog out of water.

Aoust paused the tape and lit another cigarette. It was in 1971, while gathering material for the *Encyclopedia*, that he had first heard about *Le Retour*. The older scholars he was consulting kept mentioning this interesting lost film from 1923, but apart from a few contemporary reviews and newspaper articles there was preciously little about the film itself in any of the existing scholarship, and so he had placed a classified ad in the daily papers, from *Le Monde* on the left to *Le Figaro* on the right, asking anyone who had once seen a silent film called *Le Retour* in 1923 to contact him to share their recollections for a scholarly publication, and discounting the crackpots who had shown up hoping for a free drink, his ad was surprisingly effective, especially considering that he had offered nothing in return, a testament to the deep impression the film had made on the sixteen men and one woman, ranging in age from sixty-two to ninety-three, who had responded, providing him with more than thirty hours of material so fascinating that it threatened to derail the *Encyclopedia* and consume all his energy. Nearly half a century since they had seen the film, all of the respondents could still vividly describe entire scenes, shot by shot, down to the placement of certain pieces of furniture, the quality of light, the gestures of the actors, the more dramatically inclined amongst them sometimes acting out entire episodes. Every now and then over the intervening years, convinced that there was a book somewhere in all this, Aoust would sit down and start to transcribe the material, but he never managed to produce more than a page or two before giving up in the face of the drudgery and his own uncertainty as to what to do with it all.

Turning his attention back to the tape, Aoust hit play again. Emile Rostan was describing his memories of seeing *Le Retour* at the age of twelve, making him the same age at the time of the recording as Aoust was now, though in Aoust's memory Emile Rostan was an ancient man on the verge of death. Rostan was speaking of the state of utter bewilderment he had experienced while watching the film with his father at the Vieux-Colombier, how riveted he had been by what he was seeing on the screen, how everything was jumping around, all these weird scratchy marks, dancing sticks, letters of the alphabet, thought bubbles above the actors' heads, pieces from other films, and how a horse kept walking backwards through the scenes.

Aoust stopped the tape and dug around in the shoebox until he found the Defoix tape, and holding it in his hand he thought back to that sweltering day in the summer of '72 when he made the journey to that tiny village deep in Auvergne — he could no longer recall its name — an eight-hour ordeal by train and bus, through the torpor of August. It had taken him nearly three months of rigorous detective work just to locate Defoix. He remembered how nervous he had been, walking from the deserted bus stop through the silent streets in the dead of the afternoon, holding the sweaty page he'd written the directions on, wondering what the man would be like, grateful he was alive at all. He could still vividly picture that little yellow house on the edge of the village, the overgrown hedge and the peeling fence and the bedsheets hanging limply on the clothesline in the back garden overgrown with dandelions. And when Defoix, seventy-two at the time, opened the door, Aoust thought he was at the wrong house because on some level he must have been expecting the young man of *Le Retour* to greet him, not this old man whose face was puttied over with loose flesh, his eyes without lustre, his hair gray and mostly gone, a sour old man who couldn't spare a smile for this enthusiastic young scholar who had journeyed halfway across France just to talk with him. Aoust felt again the solemnity of that house, the crucifix on the living room wall, the lace cloth draped over the television, the musty furniture and antimacassars and porcelain dogs, the thick-ankled wife pretending to make herself scarce, all the while wary of Aoust, as if he had come to tempt her husband back to perdition, the little brown Pomeranian barking at apparitions—in short, the domicile of the petty bourgeois official that Defoix had become: chief regional dairy inspector of Haute-Loire. Sitting in that claustrophobic gloom, Aoust kept asking himself if this was the right Michel Defoix. How could this be the same man who had made that remarkable film?

It was only when the wife retired to another room that Aoust summoned the courage to ask the old man if he objected to being recorded, and when Defoix said that he did not, Aoust retrieved the recorder from his bag and set it on the table between them, and the first question he asked him was, Did he know of any prints of *Le Retour* still in existence? Defoix answered that he had no knowledge one way or another of the existence of any prints, but he sincerely hoped that none had survived. Shocked by this admission, Aoust asked Defoix why he felt this way, and Defoix replied that the film was a wretched abomination, the work of a narcissist, totally devoid of any redeeming qualities. And yet he had allowed this young researcher to come and interview him, knowing full well that his ostensible purpose was to try to rescue the film from oblivion. Aoust did not say this in so many words, but judging by Defoix's awkwardness after making these pronouncements, Defoix must have sensed that Aoust was thinking it. When Aoust asked him if he himself had any elements left, the answer was an emphatic no. Aoust asked him if he was aware of how influential *Le Retour* had been to other filmmakers, how ahead of its time it was, and Defoix replied that none of that was of any interest to him. Aoust asked him if he had kept in touch with any of the technicians who had worked on the film? Again the answer was no. Aoust asked him when the last time he had seen the film was, and the answer was the night of the screening, and he had never watched it again. Aoust asked him what he had done with the work prints, and Defoix calmly replied that he had burned them, which so astonished and pained young Aoust that he audibly moaned, such that Defoix asked him if he wasn't feeling well. When Aoust told him that the Cinémathèque Française was in possession of 681 feet of the film, Defoix lamented that he had not managed to burn those as well. Changing tack, Aoust asked him if he would mind simply telling him the story that is told in the film, and Defoix said the story was stolen from Gide's *Le Retour de l'enfant prodigue*, that Aoust could read the story himself, or better yet the biblical story that it in turn was stolen from, the parable of the prodigal son, Luke 15. It had soon become apparent to Aoust that he was mistaken in believing that Defoix, in accepting his request to come and talk with him about the film, still harbored some desire for recognition, however belatedly. His true intention, in fact, was to bury the film once and for all. There was no concealed pride here, as Aoust had imagined from their brief exchange of letters. Defoix genuinely despised the film and the young man who had dared to create it; he embraced every negative opinion that had ever been written about *Le Retour*; they were all correct: it was heretical, an offense to the Church, an offense to the bourgeoisie, an offense to basic human dignity.

Listening again to the recording, to the long silences between his questions and Defoix's answers, to the grandfather clock ticking and tocking in the background, Aoust sensed a subtle change in his own feelings towards Defoix. Now that he was only twelve years shy of Defoix's age at the time, instead of nearly half a century younger, he felt he understood the man's disgust with his youth a little better. Whereas on that day Aoust had felt nothing but pity and contempt for the man, his weakness, his cowardly embrace of religion, the squelching of his talent, his life force, so much so that it had made Aoust himself begin to question the value of *Le Retour*, he could now hear in Defoix's voice the sincerity with which he had answered his questions, the generosity he had shown in accepting his request at all, and Aoust was reminded that great works of art transcend the men and women who create them, that in the final analysis what some old man thinks of the work of his youth is irrelevant—an old man had no more claims on his younger self than a complete stranger did, just as the fact that Rimbaud fled to Africa to become a businessman and disavowed by his very life the visions of his youth took nothing away from "*Le Bateau ivre.*"

Aoust listened to Defoix for a while longer, then felt an urge to hear someone talking about the sex scene. Given the stifling air of religiosity in that house, Aoust hadn't been able to summon the courage to ask Defoix himself about it, or about Nadia. He always suspected that the sex scene was the root of Defoix's disgust with the film, especially given that Defoix himself was the actor and Nadia Marinescu, his lover at the time, the actress. There came a point in nearly every interview when, their voices dropping to an astonished whisper, the respondents would begin to talk about the sex scene, conjuring from the depths of their memories the moment when the lovers moved closer together on the settee and exchanged coy glances, the woman batting her lashes and wringing her hands in expectation, the man making his own desire apparent with similar clichés, but instead of cutting to the intertitle and the next scene, as everyone expected, the scene kept going, the kiss itself shocking enough but nothing compared to the moment when the woman placed her hand on the man's crotch and started rubbing it, let alone when they quickly undressed and she started sucking him off, the frenetic white scratches on the film not so much concealing his erection as drawing the viewer's attention irresistibly to it, and then he mounted her in the missionary position, followed by six straight minutes of uninterrupted coitus, filmed directly from the side, the crackling white squiggles around their sexual organs keeping pace with the rhythm of his thrusting, the utter pandemonium it unleashed in the cinema, people rushing for the exits, people hurling chairs (those who weren't riveted to them) at the screen, the projectionist holding his ground in the booth. This was all well-documented in the newspapers of the day, the charges Defoix had faced along with his collaborators, the cinema owner, the projectionist, the print confiscated by the police, no doubt to watch in the privacy of the forensics lab.

Aoust wanted to listen again to someone's memory of this scene, to hear from the shock in their voice what it must have been like to see this with their own eyes at the Vieux-Colombier in Paris in 1923, but having no index for the tapes, it proved difficult to locate, and his ears and brain growing tired of the screel, he decided to call it quits for the day.

•

On his way back to his office after his Tuesday afternoon lecture, Aoust stopped by the mail room to check his box (payslip, teaching workshop) then carried on to sit out the first of his two weekly office hours. So rarely did a student ever avail of Aoust's office hours that he took it for granted that he could use the time to catch up on journals or attend to his procrastination of administrative matters.

In comparison to his apartment, Aoust's office was relatively tidy. Knowing that the janitorial staff came in once a week sometime in the night to empty the trash can was enough to compel him to keep the various piles of print matter and videotapes in more rectilinear assemblages to avoid anything being accidentally thrown out. He had inherited this office during the great asbestos-work reshuffle of '98 from Harriet Björnstrand, the Swedenist, who had left some of her old film posters on the walls when she was relocated to the fifth floor, telling Aoust she was graduating to a more mature aesthetic and he could just toss them. Ten years later, Björnstrand herself long since gone, the posters of young Max von Sydow and Bibi Andersson were still on the walls, not because Aoust had any great affection for them, but because on the few occasions when it had dawned on him that he should probably go ahead and take those old Bergman film posters down he could always think of something more pressing to do.

Aoust settled back in his chair behind the

desk and opened the large envelope containing the latest number of *French Forum*. At the left corner of his desk a computer monitor was vaguely discernible behind the multi-colored plumage of scribbled-over Post-it notes perpetually sprouting there since he'd stopped using his office computer around the turn of the century. For the record, Aoust was fully aware of the usefulness of computers, but, still, he didn't like them. And he especially disliked the internet. Unlike the cinema, or even television, which sucked the spectator into a world beyond the screen, the internet sucked something out of the user without transporting him anywhere. It reduced everything it touched to information. Everything was predicated on speed—pure, ceaseless acceleration. In the early days of the web he had been intrigued enough to spend hours doing searches of film databases, online archives, the requisite porn site or two, but he soon noticed that afterwards the illusion of real engagement immediately evaporated, leaving him feeling hollow and slightly sullied. While most of his colleagues didn't hesitate to join the digital revolution, Aoust decided that this was one revolution he would happily let pass him by. He did use the internet on his computer at home, a chunky old Dell laptop still loaded with Windows 98, but he tried to keep his forays into cyberspace to a bare minimum: checking his bank balance, the occasional search for an obscure actor's name. But e-mail was blessedly a thing of the past. One day five years ago, sick to death of wasting his life tending his in-box, Aoust sent an e-mail to all his contacts, both professional and personal, stating that this was the last message they would ever receive from him, explaining his reasons, reminding them that he could still be reached by all other existing channels of communication. But it soon became apparent to Aoust that e-mail had usurped all other existing channels of communication, particularly for scholarly exchange, and he felt a profound intellectual isolation descend over him when no one bothered to call or write to him, especially his fellow film scholars on the other side of the Atlantic. For the first few weeks it was as hard as quitting smoking. He couldn't escape the anxious feeling that he was missing out on important developments. To avoid temptation he closed his Hotmail account, and while it was beyond his powers to terminate his university e-mail account or otherwise eradicate it from existence, he held strong and refused to check it until, at last, somewhere in the third week, the anxiety passed and he began to feel wonderfully free. Since then it never failed to give him a glow of smug satisfaction to hear his colleagues complaining of the avalanches of e-mails they were constantly buried under. He took tremendous delight in imagining all the extra hassles that he must be constantly putting Schroft and the greater university bureaucracy to on his account, unable to communicate with him by any means other than the printed word or the telephone. But the greatest pleasure of all was being blissfully free of asinine student messages. Behind his back, and often to his face, Aoust was accused of being a Luddite, but he was indifferent to such remarks, knowing that secretly his accusers all envied him.

Aoust was tilted back in his chair, leafing through the journal, when he sensed a presence. He looked up to see the student who had been giving the speech last week in Sproul Plaza. Aoust set the journal down and turned towards the intruder. Several long seconds transpired as Aoust waited for him to announce the purpose of his visit, the three most common being: needs a letter of recommendation, doesn't like the grade he got on his essay, wants to know if he can still drop the course.

"Interesting class," the student remarked as he approached the desk.

Aoust nodded, gesturing as he did so to the chair before the desk. The arms of the student's black leather jacket creaked as he took a seat and flicked his hair aside with a quick jerk of his head. Aoust still couldn't remember the student's name and chose to avoid the awkwardness of asking him, but he did recall that his first paper hadn't been half bad. If he wasn't mistaken he had given it a B-, probably in a moment of weakness.

"I read your book," the student said.

"Oh? Which one?"

"*Shadows on the Barricades,*" he replied, holding Aoust firmly in his gaze. "So you really think a film can change the world?"

Aoust smiled indulgently. "That's a simplification of my argument."

The argument, he explained, was that the ideological content inherent in the aesthetics of the first wave of the French avant-garde, in particular the 1923-1929 period, of which a strong case could be made (and he had attempted to make it in his book) that *Le Retour* was the exemplar par excellence, had a significant impact on the core of key thinkers who would go on to lay the intellectual and political foundations of the second avant-garde (not the New Wave, he was careful to point out, which for all its pretensions to a radical politics was ultimately a commercial enterprise). The influence of *Le Retour* on these thinkers and filmmakers, as he had illustrated with numerous examples in his book, was critical to the development of cinema as a tool of radical political discourse in France, culminating in the Situationist International and other social revolutionary movements in the sixties.

The student wanted to know more about the Situationists. Who were they? What did they do? Aoust did his best to enlighten him, pleased that a student was actually interested in something other than money, sex, and sports and was seeking knowledge from a real human being rather than Google.

When Aoust had finished speaking, the student said:

"So how exactly did the world change?"

"That is not the point. The point is that it almost changed. It could have changed. Which means it can change."

Aoust looked at him.

"I saw you speaking the other day in Sproul Plaza. Are you part of a group or something?"

"Yes. The Berkeley Students Anarchists' Cooperative."

Having never heard of this oxymoronic

organization, Aoust assumed the student was pulling his leg, but when after a few more moments of staring at one another it became clear that the student was in earnest, he asked him what the goals of this group were.

"We basically believe that the entire system needs to be destroyed, and the only way to do it is by turning the enemy's best weapon, capital, back onto itself."

"And how do you do that?" Aoust asked, trying, without much success, not to sound too sarcastic.

"We stage actions against capitalist fundamentalists."

"What kinds of actions?"

"If I told you I'd have to kill you," the student said with the slightest hint of a grin.

Aoust chuckled.

"You really want to know?" the student asked.

"Sure. I'm asking."

"Just your basic cultural terrorism. Anything that wakes people up from their consumerist stupor. Anything that breeds healthy confusion, gets the adrenalin flowing, makes people question reality. Some of our recent actions have been funded by the CTA."

Aoust had no idea what that was and waited to be enlightened.

"The Cultural Terrorist Agency. They provide tactical financial support for groups like ours. You should read their manifesto. I'm sure the FBI and the CIA have a file on me. Berkeley, the home of free speech. Yeah, right."

Aoust sat pondering these revelations, not quite sure what to make of them. There was a certain flippancy in the student's voice that made Aoust wonder again if the kid wasn't having him on.

"So what kind of system would you like to see replace capitalism?"

"I have no idea. I'm no political theorist. I don't think anyone does. I don't really care, that's not my job, my job is simply to destroy the current system. There are creators and destroyers, and my job in life is to destroy."

But, as it turned out, he hadn't come to Aoust's office to talk about his mission to overthrow capitalism but simply to find out what he had missed in last Tuesday's class.

"As luck would have it..." Aoust said.

After the student had left, Aoust sat for some time thinking about all the things the young man had said, how naive he seemed, boasting of his cultural terrorism activities as if certain that Aoust would applaud them.

As hard as it was for even him to believe, Aoust had once been young and idealistic himself. He was twenty years old in May of '68, studying law at Nanterre but already in love with cinema. He had acquiesced to his father's wishes and enrolled in the Faculty of Law and Economics, with the implied understanding that someday, like his father, and his father's father before him, Aoust too would have a thriving practice of his own, preferably in commercial litigation, ensuring the perpetuity of their august name in the rolls of the bourgeoisie. Not quite Sorbonne material, he had settled for the new extension of the University of Paris, way out in the western *banlieues*. Supposedly the flagship of modernity in French higher education, Nanterre was a bleak campus of brutalist tower blocks with not a single tree in sight, bordered on the south by the housing estates of immigrant laborers, on the west by the pale gash of a motorway under construction, and on the east by the gaping trench of a planned Metro line. The Latin Quarter it wasn't. There were no common rooms or cultural facilities, the library was still being built, and worst of all the residential blocks, facing each other across a barren no man's land, were segregated: free access by the opposite sex was expressly forbidden by Paris decree and enforced by dorm wardens. If, as most historians agree, Nanterre was where the fire of the May revolution started, then thwarted desire was the spark that set it off.

In the spring of '68, Aoust was seeing a literature student named Bernadette. Like him, she had grown up in the plush middle class environs of the Bois de Boulogne but wasn't smart enough for the Sorbonne. She was tall and skinny, wore mini-skirts and glossy leather boots, and thought *Mon amour, mon amour* was a great film, though she was willing to be convinced otherwise. So every weekend Aoust drove her into Paris in his little Simca Mille to worship at the Cinémathèque Française, where thrice a night they surrendered to the divine curatorship of Henri Langlois, its eccentric director. Not every film Langlois showed was worthy of preservation, but under the spell of the imperial monumentality of the Palais de

Chaillot, its subterranean corridors lined with sacred relics of the early days of cinema, and the fervor of its devotees, everything projected at the Cinémathèque seemed like a masterpiece. After the final film, Aoust and Bernadette would drive back in raptures to Nanterre, eager to crown the night with lovemaking. But there were only so many times a self-respecting young Frenchman could deign to have sex in the back seat of a Simca, however roomy it may have been compared to a *deux-chevaux*.

Students all over France faced the same galling dilemma every weekend. It wasn't only that the Minister of Education, acting on the diktat of de Gaulle himself, treated them as if they were children, but it was as if the government didn't seem to grasp that the fifties had ended with the Fourth Republic. Students weren't even allowed to hang pictures in their rooms or rearrange the furniture, let alone engage in any kind of political activity on campus. The more radical students, seeing their unaddressed grievances as symptomatic of a pervasive paternalism, wanted to overthrow the entire government of France, if not capitalism itself.

Young Aoust, constitutionally indifferent to politics, probably would have remained aloof from all of this had André Malraux, the Minister of Culture, not sacked Langlois from the Cinémathèque in early February of that year in an attempt to exert more state control over such priceless cultural treasures—Langlois, the man who had founded the institution back in the thirties; Langlois, who had saved hundreds of films from the Nazi fires by smuggling them out of the country at great personal risk; Langlois, the godfather of the *Nouvelle Vague*. Within twenty-four hours, nearly every great director still breathing had withdrawn permission for their films to be shown at the Cinémathèque. The following Wednesday, Valentine's Day, Aoust and Bernadette ditched their classes to join the crowd of demonstrators at the Trocadéro, in front of the Palais. It was the first time Aoust had ever felt passionate enough about a cause to lend his body to it, to risk getting bludgeoned by the truncheons of the *flics*.

An armada of slate-gray CRS vans parked beneath the leafless trees made it impossible to enter the garden by the Avenue Albert de Mun. Leather-jerkined paramilitary police lined the verge, clutching their riot guns. Aoust and Bernadette climbed up on to the fountains to get a better view. A crowd of three thousand, among them François Truffaut and Jean-Luc Godard, intent on breaking the chains on the doors to the Cinémathèque, had converged near the esplanade and were chanting for Langlois' reinstatement and taunting the police. Others, arm in arm, were swaying side to side, singing "Yesterday." The opposing camps stood their ground for another half hour or so until, following Godard's lead, the demonstrators set off en masse through the garden, marching towards the entrance of the Cinémathèque. Aoust and Bernadette jumped down from the fountains and joined them, bringing up the rear. At the same moment, with a blast of shrill whistles, the wall of riot police began its advance, truncheons at the ready, visors down. The bodies collided in the middle of the garden in a cacophony of shouting and thumping. After a few minutes of mayhem, the demonstrators were routed. Unscathed, Aoust and Bernadette raced with the fleeing protestors back through the esplanade. Running down Rue Greuze, his heart throbbing with adrenaline, Aoust had never felt such ecstasy.

That same day, upon their return to Nanterre, they discovered that 450 students had occupied the women's dormitory, imposing a regime of open visitation. That night, for the first time, Aoust and Bernadette made love in her bed. By the next morning, Aoust was hooked on protest, if only in furtherance of his two great passions: cinema and sex, in that order. This handful of radical students, dubbed *Enragés* after the firebrands of the French Revolution, in league with the platform of the Situationist International, began a systematic assault on the administration of the university. They distributed ingenious leaflets in the classrooms, insulted the professors, painted provocative slogans on the walls. Aoust was intrigued by the Situationists. There was something playful about the way they conveyed their ideas — comic strips, songs, repurposed billboards — that appealed to him. They sought to foment revolution by rejecting consumerist life. This was something Aoust could relate to. He had always suspected that the benefits of modernization which his father had showered upon the family — the television, the car, the refrigerator, the vacuum cleaner — were in lieu of a deeper, more loving connection that his father was incapable of.

On the Night of the Barricades, Aoust and thirty thousand other people, no longer only students, set off from Place Denfert-Rochereau, marching towards the Right Bank. They were going to liberate the Sorbonne from the ongoing occupation by the police. There was a joyful feeling in the air, with housewives waving at them from balconies and tossing down food and bottles of wine, a sense of awakening, and yet at the same time a feeling that everyone was dreaming the same dream. It seemed that all the rules had been shattered and that humanity really was at the dawning of the Age of Aquarius, and Aoust was right in the thick of it, marching side by side with his fellow dreamers, singing the Internationale, and it was better than any drug. It was reality, beautiful reality, not a manufactured spectacle.

Late that night, after the negotiations had broken down and the battles begun, Aoust was pushed onto the sidewalk in a crush and fell among some chairs stacked against the front of a café. A cop closed in on him. He could hear the truncheons banging against the metal chairs—until a blow to the back of his skull rendered him deaf for the next few minutes. He covered his head with his hands while a hate-filled robot gave him two more blows to the back and a kick in the ribs for good measure before moving on. When he felt it was safe to do so, Aoust turned his head and looked at the street. A river of legs and shoes was flowing silently by. Framed by chair legs, and with everything drained of color in the murk of the streetlights, it was as if he were watching *Battleship Potemkin*. Only the hot slabs of pain imprinted on his body told him that what he was seeing was real, not some old silent film. Gradually, sound returned to the world, but it was no longer the world he had always believed it to be. He understood now that he was living in a world where if he dared to deviate from the path assigned to him he would feel the full power of the state crashing down on him.

Night after night through the month of May, Aoust was out there on the streets, doing his part, pulling up fencing, chopping down trees, building barricades, reveling in the camaraderie, if not quite convinced that what was happening was a real Revolution. That began to change when the auto workers at the Renault plant went on strike, then the doctors, the teachers, the sanitation workers. Every day another industry, another union, joined the strike, and it was no longer confined to Paris but had spread to the entire country. By the 23rd, ten million workers were on strike. France had been brought to a standstill. When the petrol ran out, people stopped driving. Traffic vanished from every street. No one came to drive the buses and trains. An incredible silence fell over the land. And even if you couldn't actually hear in your ears the sound of a silent factory a hundred kilometers away, you could hear it in your mind, and it only amplified the silence around you. Suddenly, people were talking to each other. No one was working. There was literally nothing else to do but converse with whoever was at hand. It was as if the country had been plunged back into the pre-industrial age. It was enchanting, a time outside of time, where the only thing that really mattered was talking.

And then, as abruptly and mysteriously as it had erupted, the Revolution was over. The workers, having won a higher minimum wage, better pensions, and a shorter work week, returned to the factories. The students decamped for their summer holidays. By some miracle, de Gaulle won the election in June by a landslide and stayed in power for another year.

●

If not for Musidora, Aoust might have been able to sleep til nine or ten on a Sunday morning, but she was not inclined to allow such a thing. She was polite enough not to jump up on his bed and curl up on his head, as Tintin, his boyhood cat used to, but she made her presence known by standing a few feet into the bedroom and meowing apologetically but insistently, letting it be understood that she expected her desires to be fulfilled, the first of which every morning was her due portion of canned food. Aoust clawed his way back to reality from the dream he was having about equipment failure during a class, got himself around to a seated position on the side of the mattress, reached for the pack of cigarettes on the bedside table, and extracted one and got it lit. Musidora had stopped meowing but remained in the same spot, following his actions with her eyes until he patted the bed and she trotted over and leapt nimbly up and settled against his leg as he smoked and petted her.

When at last he felt sufficiently awake, Aoust got up and put on his slippers and followed Musidora's sprightly footsteps to the kitchen. Opening the cabinet to the right of the sink he grabbed a can of Fancy Feast, one of the items of his weekly shopping that he gladly spent more than he needed to on, for she really did favor this brand and, money not being one of his primary concerns, he saw no reason not to indulge her. The pungent aroma assailed his nostrils as he pulled up the tab and peeled back the lid, scooping out the mealy clump with the tablespoon that permanently resided upright in the dish drainer for just this purpose.

As Musidora greedily gnawed at the moist and pungent clump of who-knew-what in her dish, Aoust took the bag of coffee beans from the freezer, dumped some into the grinder, and ground them to a fine powder. As he waited for the coffee to brew, he glanced out the window, pondering his options for the day. He wasn't sure about the Bertolucci film (*Before the Revolution*) showing at the PFA at three; he had seen it at least twice, the first time at the Cinémathèque, with Bernadette. He wasn't sure he wanted to tamper with that fine memory.

In time he got up and showered and dressed, deciding to go ahead and tackle the dishes while he waited for his sister's call. At 10:05 the phone rang and he took it and settled onto the sofa. Aoust's first question, as usual, was what had she had for dinner, for listening to Joséphine speak of food always transported him to her kitchen, a place he liked to be, if only in his imagination.

Tonight she had had a nice piece of halibut, a salad of spinach and beets picked from her own garden, some bread, a little white wine, and afterwards a very sweet orange. To her chagrin a rabbit or something had been at her chard, and sadly there was nothing left but stalks. Although Aoust had never seen his sister's house in Arles, either in person or in pictures, he could picture it perfectly from all the little details she shared with him on their weekly Sunday morning chats ever since she'd realized her dream and moved there four years ago upon retirement.

For her part, Joséphine's habitual first question was, What was Doctor Aoustus planning to do with his day? Aoust mentioned the Bertolucci film; otherwise he might walk up to Moe's, suffering the usual pangs of remorse for the demise of Cody's, maybe go to a café and read, the usual stuff. She next asked him how things were going at work, and, groaning, he told her about going to the wrong room by mistake the other day, which he was sure Schroft had gleefully filed away in her dossier against him. This name was familiar to Joséphine from previous conversations, though she didn't quite understand the nature of the problem, so Aoust had to explain to her, not for the first time, the way university departments worked, that behind the façade of liberty, equality, and fraternity they were governed, like everything else in life, by the vagaries of human emotions: ego clashes, power struggles, etc. Schroft was out for his head. Next week, for example, she was making him attend some asinine teaching workshop. God only knew what kind of nonsense he would be subjected to. It was all part of her plan to torture him into submission; which was why he needed to get cracking on his book and have a contract in hand before his next annual review.

Joséphine wasn't sure what book he was talking about, so he told her he had been listening again to all those old interviews he had recorded back in the seventies, and it had given him an idea for a book on *Le Retour*. Joséphine thought he had already written a book on *Le Retour*, so Aoust explained that *Shadows* had only touched on the film's place in the history of French avant-garde cinema, as but one link in the chain from Defoix to Debord. And knowing that when Joséphine asked questions she genuinely wanted to learn something, he told her that this book would be different; he had already written extensively on the Marxist subtext of *Le Retour*, and he didn't envision this book being beholden to any particular theoretical framework. In effect, what he wanted to do was "resurrect" the film with words. Imagine if all that remained of Picasso's *Les Demoiselles d'Avignon* was a little scrap of canvas from one corner, he told her by way of illustration, and Braque had gone on to get all the credit for Cubism. Wouldn't she want to see the missing parts, or at least have words describing them in sufficient detail that someone, if so inclined, could recreate a very close approximation of the entire painting? That was what he was going to do with *Le Retour*. While no single individual on the tapes had spoken in detail about every scene in the film, to his surprise and delight it had become apparent as he listened to the tapes again that by piecing together the interviews into a kind of collage of memories, using one person's recollection of one particular scene and another person's of another, he could effectively reconstruct the entire film, scene by scene, in chronological order. If anything, what he was attempting was closer to archaeology or anthropology than film history, letting the informants speak for themselves, with minimal authorial intrusion, revealing in the process not only the specific substance of the lost film but, perhaps more interestingly, its visceral effects on a representative sampling of the people who had seen it, exposing the contours of their individual personalities, as well as the prevailing beliefs of the culture at large, both in 1923 and, to a lesser extent, 1972. Not only would the reader of his book get a real sense of what it was like to see *Le Retour* in the theater in 1923, but also what it was like to remember it half a century later.

Joséphine was glad to hear that her brother had a new project underway, and always willing to indulge his excitement, she asked him several more questions about it, which he answered at considerable length. When he was finished she expressed her sincere hopes that his new book would help resolve his situation, though Aoust suspected that in truth his sister wouldn't be too upset if he did end up losing his job, for to her mind it would be a step in the right direction towards getting him back to France, one of her oft-spoken desires, since she knew he had been miserable for at least the last decade, maybe longer, certainly since his divorce, because he had told her so himself often enough, and she believed that coming home would solve all his problems. It was only on this matter of his hypothetical return to France that Joséphine sometimes overstepped her role as a good listener and let her own desires affect her judgement, for she didn't really understand all the complexities, having never lived in any country but France, having never married or had any children. She didn't understand that her brother, having now lived in America longer than he had lived in France, had become a hyphenated man, a Franco-American, belonging to neither country entirely, pulled farther apart from both with each passing year; he could never be purely French again, and he could certainly never be wholly American. Even if he were to return to France upon retirement, he would still be this hyphenated man, the only difference being that he would be better able to disguise it there since his French and his accent when he spoke it were thankfully still intact, which he could attest to from these weekly conversations with his sister, who, having been a school teacher for forty years and still a strict grammarian, would surely have pointed out any creeping corruptions. No, Joséphine didn't understand all the complexities, only one of which was that Michel was here.

"But you never see him," she pointed out.

"I'm seeing him Friday night. His band is playing at a club in San Francisco."

After he got off the phone with Joséphine, Aoust thought once more about what to do with his day, deciding in the end to forego the Bertolucci film, as pleasurable as he knew it would be, and go to a café to work on the book, for which he also needed to reread some secondary sources, one of which was Jean Epstein's *Bonjour, cinéma*. He found the book in record time, and shoving it into his bag, he set out for Café Milano, which came closest among the nearby cafés to satisfying his exacting conditions, although he did briefly consider Caffè Strada before deciding against it, knowing he would be distracted from his work by recollections of the real estate broker, whom he had been thinking about of late with increasing frequency. Then again, every café had its drawbacks, the most serious being the inescapable music, the omnipresent sound system pummeling the brain cells of the customers to a pulp, the incessant thumping, the beating of the hyperventilating heart of megacapitalism—that was the inescapable metaphor, for perhaps the most insidious instrument in the entire arsenal of weapons to pound one's consciousness into oblivion was the ubiquitous music, which no earplug on the market could entirely block out. There were times in the past when Aoust would politely ask the staff of whichever café he happened to be in if they could turn the music down a notch, but it never failed that it would creep back up again, until eventually he stopped bothering to ask at all, knowing that he would only come to be seen as that meddling old French guy imposing his silence on everyone. If it wasn't the café's own music, it was the throng of Hari Krishnas who always seemed to choose the moment of his most finespun lucubrations to parade up and down the sidewalk in front of the café, banging their tambourines and chanting their idiotic incantations to their god for a good ten minutes before departing. It always baffled Aoust why no one else seemed to mind the cacophony, especially the other senior scholars he periodically saw reading and writing away as if in a monastery, but that was probably because most of them were accompanied by their own private soundtracks, mainlined into their brains from their devices. And there was always the risk as well that one of his students or former students would spot him and come over to say hello, nine times out of ten to ask him if he'd seen some stupid new movie.

And yet there were times when the need to be out among the people outweighed all these objections. Aoust carried his espresso over to the only vacant table, up against the window, and took out the Epstein and began to read. Soon his mind was wandering. Maybe he actually could return, he thought, appended to which thought were the correlative memories of how happy he'd been upon his arrival in Berkeley thirty-four years ago, when he hadn't so much vowed as sensed deep in his bones that he would never return to France — not that he would never go back at all, but that he would never return for good — how he loved being singular, the Frenchman, one of the rare specimens of his kind he ever encountered on the streets, let alone in the hallways and grottos of the university; and forever entwined with these memories were the faces and bodies of women he had bedded in that two-year period before he met Helen, when he had sown his wild oats to his heart's content, the tail end of the era of free love, probably the happiest two years of his life, easiest job in the world, handsomely paid to do what he would have gladly done for free, watch films and write about them; even teaching was a pleasure in those days, before all the bureaucracy and political correctness arrived to kill off all spontaneity; not a care in the world, an eternal spring; even at the time it had seemed so, for he could still remember moments when walking across campus he would stop mid-stride, overcome by a sense of unreality, of ridiculous good fortune, overjoyed to be far from France, because the feeling of freedom was real here, not just words but something you felt in your very marrow; and after he met Helen and they married, and even more so after Michel was born, he never questioned anymore that he would never return, for he now had an American family, an American wife and an American child, and he knew that he could never get a job in France as good as the one he already had; and while Helen had always enjoyed their Parisian sojourns and sabbaticals, he knew she could never live there, for her work was here and she was American and had no particular desire to live anywhere else in the world, and of course in those days he believed he would be married to her forever, that they would probably retire in Berkeley, since he had no reason and no desire to live anywhere else. But increasingly, in the past few years, he had begun to wonder if he actually could return, if maybe he shouldn't go back. But back to what? Certain things did beckon him in moments of weakness, like the simple pleasure of being able to hear and speak his own language on a daily basis again, or the relative mental maturity of the French people, or easier access to the rest of Europe. But every time he caught himself drifting into such reveries, his rational side would point out all the problems with this little daydream, like the fact that he had no desire to live in Paris anymore — too big, too touristy — and he couldn't imagine living anywhere else in France, especially not the countryside, not Arles, because he needed to be near a cinema, and not some soul-destroying megaplex either, but a real cinema, showing real films. This was no trivial matter, for he knew all too well the states of despair he was capable of sinking into without access to a repertory cinema that screened actual, physical film, preferably 35mm, on a daily basis. So why not just stay? Was it really so important to be surrounded by people again who spoke his true language? Buñuel never returned to Spain. Gombrowicz was exiled in Argentina for twenty-two years, and when he finally did return to Europe he realized it was the biggest mistake of his life, that he had returned to his own death. But wasn't that the point? Doesn't one return in order to die, to be buried in one's native soil? Aoust shuddered at the thought of his name on a tombstone in America. But he did wish to be buried, rather than cremated, when the time came; he wanted his carcass in the ground for a couple of centuries, some place his son could visit on occasion and think a few fond thoughts of him.

As he so often did when working in a café, Aoust glanced up from his book every now and then to give his eyes and mind a break, to idly watch for a few moments the people around him or those passing in the street, students for the most part, but the rest of humanity as well, and if his eyes were sometimes drawn to a lovely young woman and lingered there longer than on other varieties of people, then he didn't deny himself the pleasure so long as it didn't impinge upon the comfort of the woman in question. That Sunday afternoon his eyes were drawn to a woman standing on the other side of the street, apparently waiting for the bus; she was young, though at first glance he would wager she wasn't a student, not an undergraduate at least; trim, healthy, not one of those gym bodies edgy with athleticism; slender legs showing below a green-patterned knee-length skirt, skin young and sleek and somehow luminous even on this overcast day; standing there with her arms crossed in front of her, her leather handbag hanging from her left shoulder, white earbud in her right ear connected presumably to a gadget in her bag, brown hair unfussed over: a "natural" woman, yes, that was what drew Aoust's eye, though he personally preferred women who wore makeup, women who made an effort to conceal something of their natural condition, kept something in reserve.

The next time he looked up from his book, Aoust noticed a man standing near the woman, slightly closer than a stranger customarily would have been, closer to her than anyone else around. Perhaps it was this that drew Aoust's eye again and caused him not to return his attention to Epstein. The man seemed like an ordinary man, but how could Aoust be sure? He could be a serial killer for all he knew. It was Aoust's distinct impression that the man and the woman did not know each other, but there was something in the bearing of the man, impossible to qualify in purely physical terms, that gave Aoust the impression that he, the man, was more than idly aware of the woman, that although he was not looking at her his attention was focused on her. It was enough to keep Aoust from looking away, this man and this woman, apparent strangers, standing a few feet apart, waiting for a bus. While Aoust was watching them, the man lifted his left hand and gently touched the woman's right shoulder, as one does when wanting to direct someone's attention to something absentmindedly dropped or forgotten — in short, a gesture drawn from the limited catalog of touch acceptable to strangers — and when she turned to him it only confirmed in Aoust's mind that they did not know each other, for there were none of the usual signs of recognition in her eyes or anywhere else on her person, no smile of unexpected delight to be encountering a friend or acquaintance on the street, only a look of expectation, as if to ask a question, not affront; nor did she pull her earphone from her ear; but most curious of all, the man's hand did not leave her shoulder but continued to rest there in a way that Aoust could only describe as tenderly, as if the man and the woman did in fact know each other after all. The man and the woman stared into each other's eyes, for how long Aoust could not say because absorbed as he was in the unfolding drama, his sense of time had evaporated, but far too long for complete strangers to be looking at each other that way, like something from a movie — that was the only comparison Aoust could make — so full of quiet drama was it; and so, despite appearances to the contrary and a lingering commitment to his first impressions, Aoust was forced to revise his initial assessment that the man and the woman did not know each other, a misapprehension revised still further when they drew together and kissed. Although it was the man who had made the initial contact by placing his hand on her shoulder, there was no mistaking that it was not simply the case of the man kissing the woman but rather of both of them kissing each other with equal desire, for not only their lips but their bodies came together, exactly as if they were two people in love.

Aoust watched this scene unfold with utter fascination and perplexity, for he still couldn't explain why, if they were lovers, the man when he initially approached her had simply stood there like a total stranger, and why after the man had placed his hand on her shoulder and she had looked at him she had not shown him the slightest sign of affection, let alone of recognition. But of course it was impossible, or at least so improbable as to warrant no distinction, that two complete strangers, prompted by nothing more than a hand on a shoulder, would turn to one another and fall into a spontaneous kiss of the deepest passion. Even with love at first sight there were stages, however brief, between the moment of recognition and the consummation with a kiss of that first flush of feeling, a moment of imbalance, of questioning, of taking stock of the situation —

Is this person feeling what I'm feeling? Should I approach her? — dozens if not hundreds of considerations playing out one after another, if not simultaneously, at the speed of thought, recognizable to even the disinterested observer as the normal human response to something as powerful as the sudden and overwhelming desire to merge with another human being. But with this man and woman there wasn't the slightest evidence of hesitation or doubt; the kiss was one of complete surrender to the irresistible force of a newborn love, though it was still unfathomable that complete strangers should fall to kissing in such a way. And yet, when the kiss was finished, the man and the woman turned away from each other once more, toward the street down which the bus could now be heard coming. The man removed his hand from her shoulder, and they returned to their respective solitudes, as if the kiss had never happened. That was the most astonishing thing of all. In whatever scenario one chose to imagine, be they former lovers or total strangers, one would expect to see the effects of such a kiss radiating through their bodies afterwards, be it an awkward daze, discomfort, rejuvenation, excitement—whatever the case, it would be evident in their movements, even to an observer fifty feet away.

Aoust continued to watch them, oblivious of the flow of traffic separating him from them, as an egret watches the play of light and shadow across the surface of the water for any sign of life below, continued to watch for the inevitable giveaway that they were in fact already lovers. But it never came. They stood apart, complete strangers again, lost in their own thoughts, awaiting the bus, which now roared and whined to a stop at the curb before them, so that for a while Aoust lost sight of them, until he saw the woman's face through the windows of the bus as she made her way down the aisle to the back. Aoust kept waiting for the man's face to likewise appear, but it never did. Other people got on, but not the man, so that when the bus finally pulled away, Aoust turned his attention back to the sidewalk in readiness to measure the man's reactions to the woman's departure, whether it be a wistful glance at the departing bus or the same strange indifference, but to his bafflement the man was nowhere to be seen. Aoust craned his head around to get a better angle westward down Bancroft, the only direction the man could have taken and escaped Aoust's notice, but the man had vanished.

Aoust sat there for some time, pondering what he had seen, trying to make sense of it, wondering if he hadn't imagined the entire thing.

•

Philip Hume, a fit older gentleman with a head like a Roman statesman, put all six attendees of the all-day teaching workshop instantly at ease with his friendliness and empathy, making it clear from the outset that none of them were there as some kind of punishment but only to explore ways of making their communication skills more effective, to build on their strengths and shore up their weaknesses, something that everyone in every profession could regularly benefit from, including himself, he assured them. He then played some videos and gave the professors reams of handouts, which they read and commented on, some more earnestly than others.

Aoust's partner-in-crime in the paired-off activities was Celia Medhurst from Sociology, and when he asked her what she had done to merit this humiliation she only smiled. Still feeling certain pleasant aftereffects from his conquest of the real estate broker, namely that given the right circumstances he still had it in him to ravish a woman, Aoust kept trying to make Celia Medhurst laugh at the sincere, self-helpish language of the handouts, which sounded even funnier in a whispered French accent, but either she felt constrained by the formality of the situation or in fact wasn't particularly amused by Aoust, for she chose not to join him in his mockery and offered only more tepid smiles.

After the lunch break, which Aoust spent alone reading in his office, the professors returned to the classroom to deliver their twenty minute practice lectures, taking on board all that they had learned in the morning. It was bad enough having to sit through John Norbury's flatulent exegesis on *The Canterbury Tales* the first time, complete with recitations in Middle English, but to be forced to watch the whole thing again on video and listen to everyone else's "constructive criticisms" was almost more than Aoust could bear. Each speaker inflicted his or her own unique brand of torture: Marc Spradlin, the historian of Medieval Europe, kept laughing at his own lame jokes that no one but another medievalist would ever have found funny; Patricia Yancey's droning monologue on ethno-racial politics was so monotonous and laden with abstruse jargon that it was all Aoust could do to keep his eyes open. When it was Aoust's turn, he got up and, doing his best to ignore the nerve-racking videographer with his camera trained on him, delivered his tried and true lecture on the grammar of silent cinema, and though he didn't really need his notes, he consulted them anyway, knowing that the results of the workshop, along with the video, were bound to be conveyed to Schroft, and he didn't want it to look like he hadn't taken the workshop seriously. Considering the pressure he was under, Aoust delivered what he felt was a fine lecture, impassioned and illuminating, perhaps a little dense here and there, especially for the scientists in the room, but on the whole a success.

Before playing back the video, Philip opened the floor to the others for comments. Celia Medhurst began the inquisition by suggesting that a little more historical context would have been useful, which Aoust dismissed as petty quibbling, given that in the actual course the historical context would have been well-established by this point in the semester, not to mention that it was just plain mean of her, considering the rapport they had established in the morning, to attack him when he had so nobly held his tongue over her own insufferable disquisition. Dan Goezler, the astrophysicist, continued the assault by pointing out, perhaps because it was Aoust who had commented on all of the "ahs" and "uhms" in his own lecture, that Aoust had a distracting habit of clearing his throat in the middle of a sentence and then abandoning the sentence altogether, resulting in big "black holes" in the flow of sense. Patricia Yancey felt he'd wandered pretty far off topic when he began telling the anecdote about Lillian Gish's driver. John Norbury agreed, suggesting the story be eliminated altogether, also pointing out that Aoust had only made eye contact six times during the entire lecture, which so incensed Aoust, the idea of this fat little pedant counting his eye movements, that he couldn't help groaning as he returned to his seat to endure the final humiliation. Two minutes would have more than sufficed to drive home the point that virtually every negative thing that had been written about Aoust in the student evaluations over the past ten years was true, but to make him suffer the entire video was cruel and unusual punishment.

Standing out in front of Dwinelle afterwards in the cool early evening air, watching all the beautiful, happy young people with their whole lives ahead of them, Aoust smoked a cigarette, which did nothing to alleviate the leaden feeling in his chest. On his way home through Sproul Plaza, he heard something that sounded like a car accident, and looking up he saw half a dozen people with metal baseball bats and sledgehammers gathered around a huge pile of what appeared to be old computers — monitors, cases, keyboards, printers — a heap of junk about ten feet in diameter slowly churning as the people pranced around it, pulverizing the pieces in a frenzy of whooping and hollering. At a safe distance from the pounders stood a loose gathering of bystanders, some watching with bafflement, others cheering particularly effective blows. As he neared, Aoust noticed a handwritten cardboard sign in the middle of the rubble that read: "Kill Your Computer!" Two campus cops were placidly watching from the front of the student union building, evidence that the demonstration, despite the appearances of an impromptu action, must have been requested, approved, and scheduled with the university. Aoust immediately thought of his anarchist student, wondering if this was one of his events, but there was no sign of him around or anything else indicating that the Berkeley Students Anarchists' Cooperative was behind this.

Aoust watched as the smashers reduced the computers to a shifting slurry of tan and black plastic awash with circuit boards, transistors, tangles of wire, shards of glass, the green and gold and pewter innards spilling out over the concrete, revealing fresh chunks not yet pummeled to smithereens, debris leaping crazily skyward and skidding away from the pile with every blow. He watched with a strange mixture of bafflement and approval, recalling that twenty years ago it had been piles of TVs that they had taken sledgehammers and baseball bats to. That message had been perfectly clear, for the television symbolized mass media and political propaganda and brainwashing and obesity and much else, but he wasn't sure what exactly these people were trying to say by obliterating old computers, for the computer, while perhaps now the primary conduit for these same evils, was a more diffuse symbol, taking in practically the entirety of modern existence, including the protesters' own means of communication. Perhaps that was the point, he thought, and the irony wasn't lost on him that many of the people cheering from the fringes were documenting the spectacle with their iPhones.

After a dinner of the remains of an Andronico's roasted chicken and two glasses of red wine, Aoust lay on his bed for an hour, staring up at the ceiling, his spirits heavy with forebodings of some vague but looming catastrophe. The last thing he felt like doing was going all the way over to San Francisco to see Michel's band, but he'd promised him he'd be there, and he couldn't back out now.

At seven o'clock he roused himself and went into the bathroom and combed some water through his hair and stared at his face for a while in the mirror and, seeing nothing uplifting there, turned away. In the living room he put the Epstein in his bag for the trip over and back, made sure he had a pair of earplugs and a fresh pack of cigarettes, checked his wallet for money and the directions he'd written on a piece of scrap paper, then he put on his dark blue windbreaker, said *au revoir* to Musidora, and set out walking to the BART station.

His spirits rose slightly as the train left the bowels of the earth after Ashby station to glide quietly along the elevated tracks above north Oakland. Sensing the change around him, he looked up from his book to see the vast blue-gray sprawl of the East Bay sliding by outside every window of the carriage, the shipping cranes of Oakland dock lined up like a cavalry of Trojan horses off to the south, the towers of the Bay Bridge jutting up in the middle distance, the long teal-blue stripe of the bay stretching from Sausalito to San Mateo, and above the water the black silhouette of the hills of San Francisco against the fading yellow dusk.

Approaching 19th Street station, the train descended again, back into the darkness, picking up speed after West Oakland as it raced with an ear-splitting roar across the bottom of the bay. Aoust returned to his book but only managed to read a few paragraphs before a cold gloom fell over his heart again. He stared out the window at the fluorescent lights streaking by like Hollywood laser beams. The last time he had seen Michel was at Christmas, when he (Aoust) had put himself to considerable trouble trying to think of a good gift for his son. He had started the process in early December, pondering here and there every few days what Michel might like, deciding sometime in the middle of the month, as he did every year, that it had to be something related to music. He wanted the gift to say what he could not say himself with words, that he supported Michel's passion if not necessarily the form it had taken, for Aoust sometimes doubted that music actually was Michel's passion as opposed to the *lifestyle* of a musician. Truth be told, Aoust had expected Michel to grow out of it during college, to realize that he wasn't destined to be a rock star, but instead of applying to masters programs, as

Aoust had hoped, after graduating from UC Santa Cruz without distinction, or starting on a career related to his degree (English), Michel had taken a job at a café in San Francisco in order to put all his energy into his band, living hand-to-mouth, borrowing money from Aoust when he couldn't make ends meet. And this was how he had been living for the past decade, working menial part-time jobs, playing the occasional gig, still no sign of any demonstrable success other than some CDs that the band themselves had paid for. Nonetheless, Aoust wanted to say with his gift that he understood his son's desire to transcend mundanity through art, but he also wanted the gift to be useful, to conceal the deeper symbolism of a father's love and understanding behind the gift's practicality.

That was probably why a pack of guitar strings, subsequently revised to an entire box of them, was the first thing that had come to Aoust's mind, though he didn't have a clue what kind of strings Michel used, or even what kind of guitar he played, and realizing that he had no way of acquiring this knowledge without giving away his intentions, he had abandoned the idea of strings, though not the idea of concealing the symbolic behind the practical. He considered an amplifier, cables, effects pedals, but in every instance the problem remained the same: he had no idea if Michel, who like all musicians was no doubt very particular about his equipment, would ever use what he got him. He briefly thought about getting Michel a gift certificate to Guitar Center, but in that scenario the symbolic value would have been rendered null by the brute practicality, and so Aoust was forced to abandon the practical/symbolic fusion and focus solely on the symbolic, which presented its own challenges, for absent the camouflage of the practical the symbolic was vulnerable to deeper scrutiny, not to mention the potential for misinterpretation, let alone the vagaries of individual taste. If, for example, Aoust gave Michel a work of art on a musical theme, a painting or sculpture or photograph depicting a musician at work, Michel might see what his father believed to be classy as simply kitschy or pretentious. Even the gift of music itself — a ticket to a concert, a video of a performance, a CD, the latter of which Aoust finally settled on as the wisest approach — was a minefield of potential misinterpretation. He had a rough idea of what kind of music Michel and his band played, assuming it was the same as the last time he had heard it, and for a while he considered taking one of Michel's CDs into Rasputin or Amoeba on Telegraph Avenue and letting the employee listen to a sample then recommend something that sounded similar, but the more he thought about it the riskier this idea seemed, for giving Michel music of the same genre as his own would only invite comparisons, most likely unfavorable, since any band that had a CD at Rasputin or Amoeba was by default more popular and successful than Michel's band. In any case, Aoust didn't like the idea of enlisting a third party into his process, for he really did want the gift to be seen to be coming from the heart—his own, not someone else's. And so he resigned himself to making the decision alone.

He was no closer to knowing what to get Michel when, several days into the impasse, with Christmas rapidly approaching, snatches of an old tune that he couldn't quite place began playing in his head. *Je roule en Cadillac dans les rues de Paris, depuis que j'ai compris la vie, j'ai un petit hôtel, trois domestiques et un chaffeur ... je vends des canons.* For some reason he vaguely associated these lyrics with May '68, but he couldn't remember any more of the song, or its name, or even who had sung it. Unable to get the song out of his head, which he interpreted as his subconscious trying to tell him something, he called Joséphine and sang, to her great amusement, the bit he could remember. Of course it was obvious the moment she told him. Boris Vian. The patron saint of Saint-Germain-des-Prés. How could he have forgotten singing along with his friends to those old Vian records on those magical nights of May? Boris Vian. France's post-war renaissance man. Engineer. Novelist. Jazz trumpeter. Music critic. Poet. Playwright. Actor. The same man who had written *L'Écume des jours*, Aoust's favorite novel as a teenager. The same man who had written, under the pseudonym Vernon Sullivan (pretending to be the book's translator from the original English), *J'irai cracher sur vos tombes* (*I Spit on your Graves*), a spoof of hardboiled American detective novels. And wasn't Vian also how Berkeley had entered Aoust's life? Aoust remembered listening to Peter, Paul, and Mary's cover of "Le Déseteur" on the radio in Paris, hearing about all the protests going on in Berkeley, California, the free speech movement, People's Park, a special place in

America where people seemed to be enlightened, so that when, five years later, he learned of an opening for an assistant professorship of French Cinema there, he flew across the ocean for the first time and poured on all his charm and landed it, only twenty-six years old, a tenure-track job in the best place in America, a dream come true. The sense of rightness that he felt as the mental giftwrapping was torn away to reveal a box set of Boris Vian CDs convinced Aoust that the quest was over.

"More Boris Vian?" Michel had quipped with irony as he tore off the paper and turned the box around to read it.

"More?" Aoust replied.

"Don't you remember you got me one of his records for like my sixteenth birthday?"

"Are you sure it was Boris Vian?"

"Yes, I'm sure. It was Boris Vian. *Alhambra Rock*. I hated it, too. All that old tinny café chanson stuff. No way in hell I was gonna listen to that around my friends. I traded it at Dave's for a Jimi Hendrix record."

The train pulled in to Civic Center station and, donning his reading glasses to consult his directions, Aoust got out and joined the Thank-God-It's-Friday throngs on the escalator up to the mezzanine level where, after some confusion with the MUNI vending machine (no round-trip tickets), he escalatored back down to the MUNI level where he consulted the signs and confirmed with an approachable-looking man that he was on the right platform for the N-Judah outbound. Two Ms and a K later, the first N pulled in, so full that only the most desperate attempted to board. It wasn't until the third N, after an interminable parade of other letters, that Aoust finally managed to board, but every seat being taken, and the thorough grayness of his beard apparently not sufficiently guilt-inducing for those younger than him to sacrifice theirs, he grabbed a handhold near the doors and rode the rocking little tram standing.

Three stops later he stepped down into the chill night air at the quiet little Noe Street stop beside Duboce Park. Again he donned his reading glasses and, stepping into the spill of the nearest streetlight, consulted his directions, which told him to head west two blocks to Divisidero, but having no idea which way west was and not wanting to start walking up the formidable incline if he didn't have to he asked another approachable-looking man which way Divisidero was. The man turned and pointed up the formidable incline. Aoust decided this was a good time for a cigarette. According to his watch it was ten after eight, meaning 8:05. Michel had said they would be going on at eight, but Aoust knew that musicians never started on time, and truth be told he didn't mind missing some of the set since in all likelihood Michel wouldn't even see him until they met backstage afterwards. A sense of calm, the pleasure of a small adventure, settled over Aoust as he stood on the sidewalk smoking his cigarette. The people who had disembarked with him were gone now, and at that moment no one else was waiting for the next tram. Not a single car was driving down the street, and behind him the park was radiating its own special frequency of silence. With each exhale, some of the lingering humiliation of the teaching workshop left Aoust's body.

It took another half hour, spent mostly waiting for a bus on Divisidero, to reach the Independent. Aoust could hear the rumbling from half a block away. A dozen or so young people in the garb of urban disaffection were loitering around on the sidewalk in front of the rust-colored building, smoking and talking. Aoust took his place in line at the tiny box office window, through which the higher frequencies of the music were flowing unimpeded. When it was his turn he leaned down to the opening and told the young woman behind the glass with all the metal on her face that his son was in the band and that he'd said there would be a ticket waiting for him at the box office. After the third attempt to understand his name, exacerbated by the hoarseness of his voice and the volume of the music behind her, she asked him to spell it for her. She studied a piece of paper for a while and told him that his name wasn't on the list. Aoust spelled it again, first and last, but it still wasn't there.

"So what does that mean?" he asked her.

"What?"

"What does that mean?" he leaned down and hollered through the opening.

"I can't let you in without a ticket."

"What?"

She said it more loudly.

Aoust thought for a moment.

"How much is the ticket?"

"Twenty-five dollars."

"Just for Venom & Eternity?"

"For the event. Both bands."

"I only want to see Venom & Eternity."

"The price is the same. There's no separate ticket."

Aoust thought again; he would be justified in turning around and going home, especially if Michel had forgotten to reserve a ticket for him.

Aoust took out his wallet and saw what he already knew, that he only had thirteen dollars cash on him.

"Do you take cards?" he asked.

Ticket in hand at last, Aoust turned and, avoiding eye contact with the annoyed people he'd been holding up behind him, made his way to the door, where the bulging bouncer gruffly checked his ticket and his driver's license and the contents of his bag, then stamped his right hand with a splotch of blue ink and waved him in.

Through the thicket of bodies crowding the dark, narrow corridor leading into the club, Aoust sidled his way forward, running the gauntlet of plastic beer cups. The music was so loud now that it seemed to be lifting him bodily off the ground and squeezing him like a python constricting its prey. He could feel the fabric of his shirt vibrating against his chest with every detonation. Emerging into the main space, he caught sight of Michel up on the stage with the other three band members, thrashing away at his guitar in a tight faded black T-shirt, dark jeans and white basketball shoes, bathed in red and blue lights spilling over onto the jutting heads and flailing arms of the denser front of the audience. Behind the band a screen was projecting what looked like scenes from Stan Brakhage films: pulsating colored abstractions resolving every now and then into brief glimpses of almost recognizable objects. Aoust squeezed his way around to the wall at the back where there was more free space and immediately began digging around in the wide inner pouch of his bag for the little plastic case with his earplugs in it. It was too dark to see into the depths of the bag, so he worked by touch alone, palping in turn his reading glasses case, the lip balm tube, three pens, his notepad, two cigarette lighters, the tissue packet and the dry erase marker, until at last he felt the small round receptacle and pulled it out. The lid was of the sort that a simultaneous upward and downward force had to be adroitly applied with one's fingertips to the overlapping flanges, and if not controlled, the sudden release could jolt the case, resulting in the feather-light earplugs leaping out and falling to the floor. Which is precisely what happened when Aoust, concentrating on keeping the strap of his bag from slipping from his shoulder, tried to open it. Cursing under his breath, a force of habit in this case wholly unwarranted given that his loudest scream would have gone unregistered in that deafening maelstrom, he removed his bag from his shoulder and set it on the floor beside him so as not to spill the rest of its contents as he bent down and started feeling around the smooth concrete floor in his immediate vicinity. He located one of the earplugs, slightly to his left, but the other one was nowhere to be felt in the small clearing between him and the shoes and boots jouncing around him, and so, cursing again, he gave it up for lost. Standing back up, he squeezed the earplug and wet it between his lips and inserted it into his right ear, the more sensitive of the two. The bliss of the diminishing volume as the earplug expanded inspired him to wad up a piece of tissue and stuff it into his left ear, and while it wasn't as effective as the lost earplug would have been, it did blunt the edge enough to allay his fears of permanent hearing loss.

In time, though not soon enough, the song ended, the audience bellowed, and the next began, equally ferocious. For the remainder of the set, Aoust stood with his back against the wall, watching his son cavorting around on the stage, screeching like a psychopath into the microphone, losing himself in his guitar. Aoust could see that it was Michel up there, but it was a Michel he could not fathom. At certain moments, in certain angles of light, when Michel's sweaty black hair wasn't shrouding his face, Aoust would catch a glimpse of the sweet little boy who loved books and nature, who liked to hide things in his daddy's beard, who was always asking questions about time and the universe, who once stood crying while an ant bit him because he was afraid of hurting the ant, the boy he used to take to Paris in the summers so he could get to know his grandparents, to see all the special places of Aoust's own childhood, to watch films together in the great old cinemas, because, as Aoust always told his son, "You aren't only American but French too." For a split second in the cold flash of the strobe light, Aoust would see this boy he knew and loved; then he was gone, replaced by this mysterious raging creature. During one of the slower songs, when Michel stopped playing the guitar and stood forlornly at the microphone pouring out his soul, Aoust was able to make out some of the lyrics, specifically the refrain, "I forgot to thank you when you killed me," and he wondered who this song was about.

Two more bombastic songs, and at last it was over. Michel thanked everyone for coming out, and he and the rest of the band left the stage. As some relatively quieter music came over the sound system, Aoust extracted the earplug and the tissue and made his way forward through the milling crowd to the front of the stage, where two stagehands were already busy dismantling the equipment.

"Pardon me," Aoust said to the nearest one. "How do I get backstage? The singer is my son. He's expecting me."

"What's your name?" the stagehand asked him.

Aoust told him, and to Aoust's surprise the stagehand didn't ask him to repeat it but instead told him to wait a minute and vanished into the wings. A minute later he returned and told Aoust to follow him, up onto the stage, around the side and back through a dingy corridor to the break room, where Michel and the rest of the band were sprawled out on a ratty olive-green sofa and some folding metal chairs, exhilarated and exhausted, drenched in sweat.

"Hey, Pop!" Michel said with evident delight when he saw his father enter. He stood up and gave his dad a sweaty hug. "You made it."

"There was no ticket for me at the box office."

"Oh, shit," Michel said. "Fuck. I totally forgot. How did you get in?"

"I bought a ticket."

"Fuck. Sorry, Dad. My bad."

"C'est la vie."

"I'll buy you dinner or something."

"Don't worry about it."

"Guys, this is my dad," Michel said, turning to the others. "Professor Aoust, cinephile extraordinaire. Ben, Neil, and Sean."

"So you're the one responsible for all our weird song titles," Sean said.

Aoust smiled.

"We met at Janine's Christmas party," Ben remarked.

"That's right," Michel said. "When you brought the Boris Vian."

"Michel's favorite artist," Aoust said facetiously to the others.

"*Michel*?" Sean said, and they all looked at Michel.

"The secret's out."

"No, I dig it," Neil said. "More original than Michael."

"You don't care about originality when you're twelve years old and fed up with all the shit about having a girl's name."

Aoust didn't know if Michel had ever officially changed it, in his passport and everything, but at least he had stopped trying to get him to call him Michael.

"What'd you think of the show?" Sean asked Aoust.

"Loud," Aoust replied, and they all laughed.

"You hungry? Grab some pizza," Michel said.

Against the lefthand wall a banquet table was set up with two open pizza boxes, a bag of corn chips, bottled water, a few beers, a bottle of vodka and some Cokes.

"That's some of our new shit," Ben said.

"Pretty good crowd," Neil remarked.

"Yeah, but what was up with that freaky chick in the rabbit ears?"

"She was totally wasted."

"I saw you at the back," Michel said to his father.

"Did you? I didn't think it was possible."

"You can see everything when you're up there. All your senses are on fire. You pick up on every little energy shift in the audience. I saw you putting earplugs in."

Again everyone laughed.

"Yes, well," Aoust said, playing along good-naturedly, "I assure you I could still hear every piece of shrapnel flying past my head."

Michel patted his father on the shoulder and grabbed a piece of pizza.

"I seriously fucked up the G-sharp in the bridge on 'Cocktail,'" Sean remarked.

"I liked that jazzy camouflage thing," Neil said. "Doo-twang."

"Kinda Floydy."

"Meat Puppetty."

"Get something to drink, Dad."

"No, I'm fine."

"A beer?"

"No, thanks."

"That one song," Aoust said to Michel while the others carried on talking about the gig and various aspects of their performance, "the slow one, something about 'I forgot to thank you for killing me...'"

"'I forgot to thank you when you killed me,'" Michel said.

"Who's that one about?"

"No one in particular."

"You weren't thinking of anyone when you wrote it?"

"It's about breakups. Girls."

"I see." Aoust nodded. "I liked that one."

"Thanks."

"I couldn't hear the lyrics on the rest of them."

"Not when you're wearing earplugs, you can't."

"It wouldn't have made any difference. The instruments are too loud, and you don't really enunciate when you're singing."

"Yeah, enunciation's not real big in Metalcore."

"But don't you want people to know what your songs are about? You write the lyrics. They mean something to you. Shouldn't they be heard?"

"The kind of people who listen to our music understand them. If not they can always look them up on-line."

"Tell me some of the lyrics."

"Come on, Dad."

"Humor me. Give me a few lines from one of the songs I heard tonight."

Michel poured some vodka into a glass and filled the rest of it with Coke. He looked at his father.

"'Set fire to the stars in your eyes, before you burn out and lose sight, before you break down, before you break down and bite the wire, a life consumed in the twilight of an empire.'"

"See? I would've liked to have been able to hear those words. They're interesting. Is that something political?"

"We're not trying to change the world, Dad, we're just communicating."

"But what are you communicating, just a bunch of feelings? Undirected anger?"

Michel took a drink.

"How's classes?" he asked.

Aoust took the hint, deciding this probably wasn't the best moment to start grilling Michel about the meaning of his songs. Instead he told him about finally starting to transcribe those old Defoix tapes, and how tedious it was.

"I spent six hours on one tape yesterday, and I'm still not finished with it. I thought I could get it done over spring break. Now I don't know."

"Why don't you just get some voice recognition software for your computer, let the computer do all the hard work?"

"It's all in French."

"So what? There's French programs, I'm sure."

"It would never work with these tapes. They're those tiny microcassettes. The sound is horrendous. All kinds of street noise. Wind. Broken words. Homophones. Besides, I get ideas about the book while I'm typing."

"Is it going to be in French or English?"

"English."

"So you have to translate it all, too?"

"That's the easy part."

"Oh, before I forget, here's one of our new CDs," Michel said, grabbing one from a cardboard box in the corner and handing it to his father. The cover art was a black-and-white image of what appeared to be a volcanic explosion billowing clouds of ash, one protrusion of which looked like a baby's scrunched-up face. "Venom & Eternity" at the top in scary black letters. At the bottom, smaller, but equally scary: "Burnt Offerings."

Aoust turned it around and tried to read the song titles on the back, but the font was too small.

"So this is new stuff?" he asked.

"Yeah, most of it. It's been about a year in the works."

"Are you happy with it?"

"I think it's our best album yet."

"Good. Good."

Aoust put it in his bag.

"Well, I guess I should get going."

The other three, hearing this, turned their attention back to him.

"Aren't you sticking around for Thought Crusade?" Neil asked.

"What's that?"

"The headliners. Great band out of Chicago."

"Never heard of them," Aoust said, and they chuckled, he wasn't sure why. "I should be going," he said to Michel. "I've got a long voyage ahead of me."

"How'd you come?"

"BART, MUNI, bus, foot."

"Why don't you just take a taxi back?"

"Waste of money. I've already got my BART return. Besides, how often do I get a chance to walk around the city at night? It's a different world over here."

Aoust said farewell and congratulations to the rest of the band.

"Thanks for coming out, Pops."

"I enjoyed it," Aoust said, only realizing at that moment that he actually had.

•

Holed up in his apartment over spring break, Aoust worked day and night transcribing. Even when he was on a long, smooth stretch of perfect audibility it was a slow and laborious process. Having first listened at length to a substantive section to get a sense of the trajectory and to train his ears to the idiosyncrasies of the speaker, he would then rewind and start breaking it down into five-second segments, pause the tape, type the words into the computer, then carry on with the next five-second chunk. On a good day he could get through ten minutes of speech, roughly four typed pages, before his brain became too fried to continue. But more often than not he found himself tangled for hours on end in the convoluted thickets of living speech, which obeyed virtually none of the rules of the written word, going over the same thorny patches again and again in an effort to understand not only individual words and phrases, but the meaning of entire paragraphs unencumbered by the niceties of punctuation. When not hindered by the oratorical shortcomings of the speaker — mumblings, poor enunciation, changing words mid-thought, changing thoughts mid-word, searching for the right word and failing to find it, leaving words and phrases unspoken under the assumption that the interviewer knew what he meant, drifting off into long, irrelevant digressions in the middle of which a solitary snippet of sense might lie marooned, inopportune laughter, coughing, clucking, sighing, snorting, wheezing, whistling, groaning, and other verbal tics too numerous to catalog — Aoust also had to contend with all manner of atmospheric disturbances consistent with a substandard recording from the terrasse of a bustling Paris streetside café in 1972, forcing him to rewind across the section in question again and again, trying to fathom the phonemes.

The one question that all of the voices seemed to be asking, without expressly doing so, was, Who the hell was this man who had made this film? In the process of transcribing the Defoix tape, of listening with intense concentration and typing every single word, Aoust realized several things — in actuality he had realized these things previously but had forgotten having done so — which supported his long-held belief that Defoix's choice of the prodigal son story was not accidental, that *Le Retour* was in fact largely autobiographical. It stood to reason that the story that a young man, only twenty-three years of age, should feel most compelled to tell would be the story of his own life. (That the name of the film's protagonist, played by Defoix himself, is Michel, was only the most obvious self-indulgence.) In response to Aoust's questions about his childhood, Defoix had revealed that at the age of eleven he was taken out of school by his father to do the housework. Aoust hadn't given sufficient thought before, or so he thought, to the fact that the only reason a male child in rural France in 1911 would have been taken out of school to do housework — not farmwork, but housework, *"le ménage"* — was if there were no mother in the picture. Evidently the mother mentioned in the obituary had either died during Defoix's childhood or was otherwise absent from his life from an early age. Aoust also knew from things Defoix said elsewhere on the tape that, again as in the prodigal son story, his only sibling was an older brother. This, along with certain subtle intimations in Defoix's voice, only confirmed Aoust's conviction that Defoix wasn't simply doing a modern take on the prodigal son story with *Le Retour*; he was telling his own life story, however disguised behind all the surrealism and technical virtuosity.

That story went something like this: sometime in 1922, having finished his military service and returned to his family farm in Burgundy, Michel Defoix, seeking a better life, left his childhood home for good, leaving behind his father and older brother, and made his way to Paris. Whether he traveled by bus, as in the film, or got there by other means, is unknown. It is probably safe to assume, however, that unlike the film's Michel, Defoix did not enact one of the classic tropes of parables and allegories and clandestinely sell one of his father's cows, but in all likelihood he would have arrived in the city with a certain amount of money garnered one way or another from his father's holdings to sustain him until he found a job. Aoust knew from the Jean-Louis Croze interview with Nadia Marinescu (*Cinémonde*, 4 December 1928) that Defoix was working at the bistro Monsieur Paul when she met him — she had made much of the fact that the first job a young man named Michel should get upon his arrival in Paris was on Place Saint-Michel, a stone's throw from Pont Saint-Michel — and Aoust also knew from Jules Méline's ("26-10-72 – Paris") recollections of several lost scenes that the bistro where the film's Michel works is the same Monsieur Paul; Jules Méline was absolutely certain of this because he had frequented Monsieur Paul himself from 1920-22, when he worked as a cook in the commissary of the Préfecture de police just across the river; he recognized the façade of the bistro in the scene where the thug whom Michel owes money to waits outside for him on payday to collect, leaving him barely enough to survive. Méline also remembered the chubby-cheeked bartender (playing himself) who in another scene crawls out of a trapdoor in the floor with half a dozen kittens in his arms. The distorted shots of drinkers, the barmaid's resigned exhaustion as she wipes the bartop, Michel's timid desire in following her to the wine cellar—all of these images were vivid in Jules Méline's recollections. As for the rest of the film's story — the sequence with the prostitute, the drinking and gambling, Michel living in the slum dwelling — it was impossible to know how much, if any of it, actually happened to Michel Defoix, whether it was stolen from Gide, as Defoix himself had claimed, a loose interpretation of the biblical story, his own experiences, or some combination of all of the above garnished with pure imagination. Aoust also had to concede that the ending of the film, the long walk back to the family farm, the tearful embrace with the father, could not have been autobiographical, unless prophetic, for the simple reason that Defoix himself did not leave Paris until more than a year after the disastrous screening. Whether or not there was a similar scene of reconciliation with his father and brother was impossible to say, but Defoix's subsequent life in Auvergne, as revealed by the trappings of his home, his embrace of Catholicism, his choice of profession, was in essence a return to the world of his father. In a very real sense, whether by some quirk of fate or by his own volition, Defoix's life seemed to conform in broad strokes to the story of the prodigal son.

For Aoust, one of the most abiding mysteries in the life story of Michel Defoix was, How in God's name did this barely educated son of a dairy farmer come to make one of the most radical experimental films in the history of cinema? It was safe to say that virtually none of the innovations of *Le Retour* had come about through intellectual engagement with the prevailing theories of the French avant-garde cinema. Defoix had such little knowledge of film production that, according to Marinescu, his original plan had been to shoot the entire film in sequential order, doing all the editing in camera, believing that this was how films were made. What events in Defoix's life could have possibly led him to believe that he had the ability to direct a film, let alone the wherewithal to muster the technical, financial, and creative resources to actually do so?

One memory that Defoix speaks about on the tape with some feeling, when Aoust asks him about formative cinema experiences, is a film he saw in the tent of a traveling carnival when he was nine years old. One night he and his brother sneak off of the farm and run to the village with only two francs between them to see the carnival. Once there they decide to spend their money on what the barker promises to be the journey of a lifetime, and finding a place in the clearing of dirt in front of the chairs, they are transported to the fabled city of Paris, *la Ville-Lumière*, where they see bustling boulevards, sparkling arcades, ladies in fancy dress, horse-drawn fiacres, omnibuses and trams, velocipedes and underground trains, restaurants, buildings like wedding cakes, everything shining as if through a crystal ball, and when the film is over and they emerge from the tent and he sees the stars in the night sky, smells the grass and the onions and tomatoes in the nearby fields, hears the crickets and the music of the carnival and the men and women talking and laughing, he feels drunk, though he isn't staggering, rather a floating sensation, as if he could fly, and he wants to be alone with this feeling, away from his brother, so he tells Jacques he'll be home in a minute and takes a walk and lets the stillness of the warm summer night soak into him. Only hours later when the feeling begins to fade and thoughts return of tomorrow and his father and brother does he return home.

So powerful was this stock novelty film's effect on Defoix that he recreated the entire experience in one of the early scenes of *Le Retour*, as attested to by Nadine Fernex ("18-09-72 – Paris"), the only woman who had responded to Aoust's ad and the only respondent who remembered the carnival scene. Perhaps even more so than the sex scene, this was the one lost scene that Aoust could bring himself nearly to tears lamenting he would never see. Remarkably, the very same tone of magic conveyed by Defoix was echoed in Fernex's enchanting voice as she remembered watching this scene at the Vieux-Colombier as a young woman not long in Paris herself. Listening again to this charming old lady, now all but a memory herself, Aoust marveled at the persistence of emotion, how the essence of Defoix's childhood experience seemed to survive virtually unchanged its translation into art, its absorption into the memories of another human being through cinema, its further transmutation via language nearly half a century later into another person's subjectivity, and another four decades on it still glowed with its original warmth through the hiss and whir of a barely audible recording, the magic conceivably able to survive even its impoverishment to a paragraph in an academic text to be published at an as-yet-unknown date in the near future. Magic this strong could only have been born of lived experience.

But of course it was the sex scene that all the respondents remembered most vividly. Fifty years after their one and only viewing of the film, each respondent brought to their recollection of this scene a lifetime of their own sexual experiences, so that what they claimed to remember was perhaps more revealing of their own predilections than what they actually saw that night in 1923 at the Vieux-Colombier. While six of the respondents clearly remembered the actors having sex in the missionary position, the rest of them clearly remembered something altogether different: Jean Queuille, *"le 69,"* Max Roclore, *"la levrette,"* Paul Mermaz, *"contre le mur,"* Victor Noulens, *"l'enclume,"* Claude Gardey, *"le sphinx,"* Edgard Boulin, *"le noeud coulant,"* Georges Chapsal, *"en l'air,"* Henri Thellier, *"la cuillère,"* Robert Rochereau, *"le foetus,"* Léon Mangon, *"le cheval à bascule,"* Maurice Ruau, *"la victoire."* They all recalled the weird white squiggles censoring the sexual organs, but Fernand Dariac recalled the scene taking place in a meadow while Albert Gadaud remembered it in the narthex of Sainte Chapelle; Emile Rostan recalled a chambermaid joining the action while Pierre Faye remembered there being a dog present, jealously watching the proceedings. All these variations presented a conundrum to Aoust: the *Paris-Soir* article (24 November 1923) clearly states that the actors proceeded to engage in coitus *"dans la position du missionnaire,"* and this report being the most proximate in time to the actual screening, Aoust had to accept it as the most reliable; but for this book Aoust was less interested in dry journalistic facts than in the dynamic and, admittedly, fallible reconstructions of human memory, and so he chose to include them all.

The loss of the sex scene was particularly painful to Aoust because it was perhaps the most nakedly autobiographical scene in the whole of *Le Retour*. Although more was known about Nadia Marinescu than Michel Defoix, since she went on to act in other films, Defoix's relationship with her remained clouded in mystery. By her account she met him sometime in the summer of 1923. She does not elaborate in the Croze article on the nature of their first encounter, only that it was at Monsieur Paul, or how it came about that they decided to make a film together, but it was well-established that Nadia had been acting in pornographic films since at least 1921 under the direction of Natan Tannenzaft, a Romanian homosexual Jew who became a French citizen, changed his name to Bernard Natan, and later became head of Pathé Studios. At least three of Natan's single-reel stag films that Nadia acted in — *Les Filles de Loth* (1921), *Un apéritif bien servi* (1922), and *Le Beau Champignon* (1922) — shown in private clubs in the Paris-Lyon-Marseilles axis, had survived, providing incontrovertible evidence of Nadia's involvement in France's illicit film trade in the early 1920s.

It was from the great Henri Langlois, still the Director of the Cinémathèque Française in 1971, when Aoust was just starting to get interested in *Le Retour*, that Aoust had learned of Nadia Marinescu's connection to Bernard Natan, and it was also Langlois who had told Aoust that the penis sticking up from the pile of leaves in *Le Beau Champignon* belonged to none other than Michel Defoix. Langlois claimed to know this on the good authority of his mother's sister, who had been a make-up artist at Opéra Films in 1929, when Nadia had a minor role in *Un soir au cocktail's bar*, her final film. One night after filming, Nadia got drunk with Langlois's aunt and told her about the sordid past of Bernard Natan, who was producing the film and who in his long quest for bourgeois respectability had just acquired Pathé's production and exhibition divisions. Langlois's aunt didn't believe her, so Nadia, who was suffering from severe depression and aching to reveal her own disreputable past to someone, told her that she knew these things for a fact because she herself had "acted" in dozens of Natan's films. Unburdening herself, Nadia poured into this poor woman's ears the principal extract of her anguish, her belief that she had destroyed a beautiful young man, seduced him at the behest of Natan, who needed fresh meat to perform in his films, lied to him, told him she loved him, promised it would only be one time, just to help him get out of debt, and going against all his better instincts the young man had acquiesced, under one condition: that his face not be visible in the film. This was the origin of the scenario for *Le Beau Champignon*. In that film, spotting a lone woman gathering mushrooms in the woods, a man buries himself beneath leaves, exposing only his penis for the woman to discover. Poking through the leaves, the circumcised penis looks very much like a mushroom, but the randy woman puts it to more traditional use. The name of this young man, Nadia told Langlois's mother, was Michel Defoix, with whom she would subsequently have the honor of making a real work of art.

The only part of this story that Aoust had been able to corroborate was that Nadia had indeed acted in at least three pornographic films, including *Le Beau Champignon*. Aoust owned a bootleg videotape of that film, and many a time had he watched it over the years, pondering the nature of the relationship between Nadia and Defoix.

It always saddened Aoust to think what might have been if only Defoix had had the courage of his convictions, if he had pressed on with his vision instead of destroying *Le Retour*, if he and Nadia had made more films together. Perhaps if he had stuck it out for another ten or twenty years, Michel Defoix would have eventually been fêted by the doyens of the French avant-garde as the genius that he was. And Nadia might have become another Musidora, starring in prestigious art films that questioned the prevailing power structures, rather than playing minor roles in bourgeois confections that only reinforced the assumptions that class was immutable and that the rich were so by right; her strong accent as she ventured into sound films might have been viewed as an asset rather than a liability; she might not have slid into alcoholism and depression; she might not have ended her life, alone and forgotten, in a flea-ridden hotel room in Montmartre on August 3, 1929, by an overdose of Veronal.

Aoust looked at the clock and was astonished

to see that it was well past two in the morning. He stood up and stretched his aching back. He had to get out, get some fresh air. He put on his jacket, checked for his wallet, his cigarettes, the lighter. He saved his work and turned off the computer. His stomach was sour from too much coffee. The sound of the squealing rewind seemed to linger in the air, following him down the stairwell and out onto the quiet street. He considered taking a walk through campus but thought better of it at this time of night. Practically every week in the *Daily Cal*, which despite its narrow remit and amateur reporting he always enjoyed reading, there was an article about someone being mugged or assaulted or raped in some dark corner of the campus, usually women, but a man obviously past his prime would also be an easy target.

He lit a cigarette and walked down Dwight, then turned left onto Fulton, thinking he would walk to Ashby and back and call it a night. As he crossed Parker Street he glanced up and noticed something peculiar transpiring in the middle of the street about halfway down the block. A streetlight was shining at the far end of the block, otherwise the street was dark, so it was hard for him to discern precisely what he was seeing. He stopped and narrowed his eyes. Two people, seemingly dressed all in black, neck to toe, or if not black then something dark, were standing a short distance apart, facing each other lengthwise along the street so that one appeared a little to the side of the other and slightly farther back. They were poised in nearly symmetrical postures, each with one arm straight aloft near the side of their heads, the other arm down tight against their thighs. The positions of their hands, the upper one perfectly vertical, the lower perfectly horizontal, along with their stiffly shuffling legs and periodic side-to-side head movements, called to mind a King Tut dance, or perhaps a minimalistic Tango. After a while the far one slowly swung around with mincing steps, and the other followed suit so that now they were facing each other crosswise about six feet apart, all the while keeping their arms and hands in those evocative postures, not so much echoing each other as anticipating and moving simultaneously, as if they were responding to the same inaudible piece of music. There was something both enchanting and sinister about their perfect synchronicity, something mantis-like about their rigid adherence to each other's movements, out there in the dead of night on a dark street in Berkeley, performing this silent mating ritual for no one but themselves. Maybe they were thieves, Aoust thought—the dark clothes, the precision of their movements. Could it be that he was witnessing the preparatory stages of some daring larceny? Again thoughts of the anarchist student entered his mind, though how this bizarre pas de deux could possibly be related to "waking people up from their consumerist stupor" he had no idea. Now they were moving laterally across the street with those same Geisha-like steps, still maintaining the same postures, still keeping the exact same distance between themselves, as if connected by some strange magnetic force. The one in the lead, walking backwards, stepped up onto the curb, and a short while later the other repeated the move. Then they vanished into the shadows of the trees.

Aoust waited a moment to see if they would reemerge and continue their spooky little Tango, but they didn't. Dropping his extinguished cigarette and needlessly grinding it out with the sole of his shoe, he carried on walking, staring all the while into the shadows into which the mysterious duo had disappeared. There was a house nearby with a light on inside, but the curtains were drawn, and he could see no movement within. Aoust stood listening, staring across the street, but he could hear nothing save the chirps of a solitary cricket and, somehow, the faint echo still in his ears of the screeling microcassette player. Beside him, parked roughly where he had first noticed the two people, was a white van with black writing on the sides and back. Suspecting a link between the people and the van, he stepped closer to read what was written on it, half expecting it to be the name of a dance troupe or some other branch of the performing arts.

"East Bay Glass," it read. "Since 1923. Your Local Glass, Window & Door Manufacturer & Installer."

•

Out in front of Dwinelle, set up near the benches where he could catch the maximum of student traffic, Stoney Burke was holding forth on Republicans and other idiocies of American life. He had been doing his little performances on campus every Tuesday for as far back as Aoust could remember. Plumper and balder than in days of yore, he was wearing baggy blue clown pants held up with suspenders, a black-and-white striped jailbird shirt topped by a bow-tie, and a San Francisco Giants ballcap, wisps of white hair tinted blue sticking out over his ears. On the ground before him lay an open suitcase with newspapers and various other props spilling out onto the pavement.

Not wishing to be engaged or become the butt of a joke for not engaging, Aoust veered off to the right of the small cluster of students gathered around Stoney, but it wasn't far enough.

"Hey, it's Karl Marx!" Stoney barked in his perpetually hoarse voice. "Love the beard, Karl. How's classes?"

Aoust carried on walking without acknowledging the comment. Stoney blew two short blasts on his cop whistle and continued with his shtick.

"Karl and I go way back. Thirty years and I've never gotten to second base with him. Speaking of Marx, the shit that's going on these days, my God. You know what's going on, right? Real estate bubble? You've heard of this real estate bubble, right? Biggest fuckin bubble in the history of the world, makes the tulip bubble look like, like, like a fuckin tulip bubble."

Aoust stopped about twenty feet away, out of the range of fire, and stood for a while, listening.

"If I print money in my own home it's called counterfeiting, if an accountant does it it's called cooking the books, but if a banker does it it's perfectly legal, right? Legalized fraud. These bankers peddling rotten mortgages all over the fuckin country, selling this shit to banks all over the world, betting they're gonna fail cuz they know they're rotten, placing bets with insurance companies, insuring themselves against the failure of the shit they're peddling! When this shit goes down it's gonna make the Great Depression look like the good old days. Remember, Stoney said it, right here at UC Berkeley. What's the date today? April first. That's right, April Fools' Day. Happy April Fools' Day, everybody! The day that never ends in America. Shit, I could be getting rich, short the housing market, invest the thirty-eight dollars I have in my savings. You're gonna have a fuckin revolution on your hands when all that money evaporates. I wish. You know what's gonna happen? The Fed's gonna bail out these banks. April Fools! You watch. Socialism for the rich, capitalism for the poor, fuckin global Ponzi scheme. Dark days, my friends. We're all debt slaves now, slavery never ended, it doesn't matter what color you are anymore, we're all slaves, brother, ha ha. Friedman, the Chicago school, Reagan, Thatcher, deregulation, thanks folks, get rid of the rules, get rid of Glass-Steagall, yeah, great idea, might as well just go to Vegas, set up congress at Caesars Palace, better odds. Wake up, people! Take the red pill! Viva la revolution, man!... Hi, how you doing today? Happy April Fool's Day. You just get here? Step right up. It's eighteen dollars and fifty cents apiece. This is another Cal event... Oh, man. Dark times. You know I was out here thirty years ago, before the computers, before the cameras, before the iPods, the iPhones, every spot down here had another street performer. This was my spot, under Sather Gate was another, out at the edge of the campus was another, middle of Sproul Plaza was another, those were prime spots. Who's left now? Me and Yoshua. That's it. Remember repertory theaters? The UC Theater? People used to go to theaters and watch films together, that was beautiful. Remember when we had bookstores? People went to bookstores, to look at and feel the books in their hands, it's all gone. Someday you're gonna come to campus, there's gonna be an iPhone sitting right here on a platform and I'll be on it, talkin shit, and they'll say, finally they've gotten everything, Stoney's now in the iPhone 12, on a Verizon wireless mindfuck wave. Remember the days when Stoney used to come out here live, in person, say 'fuck' out loud. Fuck! Fuck the president, stop the war. Remember when he was the only guy who said stop the war more than six times on any given day while these little snotballs walked around in their tourist uniforms, taking in the sun and a major along the way. Remember when the campanile was shorter? Remember when the football coach didn't make more money than the last six presidents of the United States? I've got the scoop on everything, goddamn! I've been brainwashed like everybody else. Like it matters. At least you're watching me instead of TV, or a computer, and believe me, I know that when you're watching me you're thinking about sex..."

Aoust turned and carried on walking home. After dinner, not eager to get back to work on the transcribing, and dreading even the thought of reading the student essays, he watched *Les Liaisons dangereuses 1960* on VHS, which he had bought in a burst of sentimentality at the Ashby flea market for fifty cents fourteen years ago, remembering when his father for some unfathomable reason had taken him to see it at Le Grand Rex when he was eleven years old, how bored he'd been after he'd eaten all the chocolate. Watching it again after all these years he was surprised by how good it was, particularly Thelonius Monk's score, but this pleasant surprise paled in comparison to his astonishment when he learned in the credits that the man with the long face and regal nose and penetrating eyes who played Prévan and whom Aoust knew he had seen before but couldn't remember where was none other than Boris Vian.

Aoust went to the phone and dialed Michel's cell number but got put straight through to voice-mail. He hung up before the sound of the beep.

Still not disposed to start reading the dreaded student essays, he decided to do a little more transcribing instead. Listening to Georges Chapsal ("16-05-72 – Paris") talking about the violent response of the crowd on the night of the screening, Aoust couldn't determine if, in one particular sentence, Chapsal was saying *la maire* or *la mère*. It didn't help that a car's horn had obliterated the article. He rewound the tape and listened again, holding the machine against his ear to try to unravel the meaning from the surrounding context. Chapsal was describing how a mob, intent on destroying the film, had tried to break into the projection booth. Aoust rewound again. He listened a few more times, rewound. He stopped the tape and sat there in silence. He couldn't go on. He realized that if he had to listen to any more of that screeling he would go insane.

He tried calling Michel again, but again it went straight through to voice-mail.

On the desk, beside the full ashtray, lay the real estate broker's card. He picked it up. *Margaret Perkins.* An address in Fremont. Two phone numbers and an e-mail address. Aoust sat holding the card, succumbing to the flow of impressions all jumbled together in no apparent order in his mind: his first sight of her naked body, its amplitude, not the most appealing aesthetically, not to his taste at all in fact, yet her comfort in it, her apparent indifference to her own body, which somehow nullified his aesthetic objections, that inane request in the theater, the perfume, cheap in his mind regardless of its actual cost, and yet that moment of shared enchantment at the end of the film, the lingering magic in the evening air, the shocking force of his orgasm, which left him partially paralyzed for a good ten seconds. Surely this was the only reason he was still thinking about her at all, this orgasm, weighed against all her flaws, symbolized in these fleeting recollections by the excesses of her flesh, her thicknesses, but again counterbalanced by a certain levity, a lightness of spirit, a certain freeness about her, open to new experiences, a levity concomitant with a lack of depth, the American happy-go-lucky nature, oblivious of its own violence. How genuine was her apparent delight in *Le Retour* anyway? Who was to say she hadn't been putting on an act, responding to the vanity he'd displayed during his introduction of the Rodier film?

Aoust stared at the card. No, he was certain it had simply been a rare confluence of factors: the film, the weather, the fragrance of jasmine in the air, the novelty of having a woman in his apartment. Why was he thinking about her at all? He wasn't in the market for a girlfriend. He was done with American women, probably done with women altogether. He was never going back to that; he'd done his time, twenty-four years in harness; he wasn't about to give up his freedom. And yet, here he was holding her card, contemplating calling her. It chagrined him a little that he had performed so poorly, not so much for her sake as his own, for if it truly was his last sexual conquest, as he deemed it very well could be — at his age how many more opportunities like that was he going to get? — he only wished he had been able to prolong it a little, to savor the moment for a few more minutes rather than crying out in that silly way after a few desperate thrusts, but it had been so long, so so long. How many years? At least two years before the divorce, add that to the ten—twelve years without sex! And he had scarcely masturbated in all that time either, so little pleasure did even that give him anymore, the mere thought of it depressed him, and to feel this big, meaty woman, to see all that flesh on top of him, it had all been too much.

Aoust picked up the receiver and dialed the number.

Six rings later she answered.

"Hello?"

"Hi, is this Margaret Perkins?"

"Yes? Who's calling?"

"Hi, this is Professor Aoust. We saw *Le Fils prodigue* together at the PFA in Berkeley."

"Hey there! I thought I recognized your voice. How's it going?"

"I was just calling to see if you'd be interested in seeing a film at the PFA tomorrow night."

"Darn. I wish you'd called sooner. I've already got plans for tomorrow night."

"Well, maybe some other time," he said, eager now to get off the phone.

"Are there any more good films coming up? That was such fun."

"There's always something good at the PFA."

"We should do dinner too. Let's see, what is today? I'm just trying to think. It's hard for me to book. Can I get your number?"

Aoust gave her his home number, changing the final digit on a sudden, irrational impulse.

"Is that your cell?"

"I don't have a cell phone."

"Wow! I don't think I've heard anyone say that in a long time."

After they hung up, Aoust sat there replaying the conversation in his mind, analyzing her chirpiness, her peculiar lack of acknowledgement of the sex. *Fun*. It had all been a meaningless lark for her. Did she sleep with every man who was willing? He was sure she was just making excuses, probably cheating on her husband. He couldn't remember if she'd been wearing a ring. She had gotten her novelty, her night with a Frenchman, and she didn't need any more. It was probably the apartment that had put her off, women have no stomach for disarray. All she'd wanted was a quickie. She hadn't been the least interested in Defoix, she'd only been humoring him to get him in a supine position with his cock up her. It was all clear to him now. His first impressions had been right. One should always go with one's first impressions. It annoyed him that he was thinking these thoughts at all.

•

"Finally you answer," Aoust said irately upon hearing Michel's actual voice on the other end of the line. "I've been calling and calling. I need you to help me try to get one of those transcription programs."

"Sure, Dad, but you'd never be able to use it on that old computer."

"I don't want a new computer. I've got all my stuff on this one. I have it all set the way I like it."

"It'll never work. You need at least Windows 7, 64-bit."

"Why can't I just put that on my computer?"

"Trust me, it won't work."

"That means I'll lose my word processing program. All my settings. I don't want the internet and all that stuff."

"You've got to get over this fear of the internet, Dad."

"It's not fear, it's repulsion."

"Whatever it is, it's a huge pain in the ass."

For the next fifteen minutes, Aoust kept up a constant barrage of questions, at the end of which it was decided that he would get the new computer but only use it for this job.

Michel picked him up around two on Saturday in his 1982 Datsun 210 station wagon, the same car he'd been driving since college. The car was already old and battered when Aoust helped him buy it for eight hundred dollars in 1995 from a middle-aged woman in El Cerrito. The Beast, as Michel called it, initially in reference to its lucky license plate number (1UZM666) but in due course to its diabolically eternal life, was the indestructible car, once bright yellow but now the color of rancid milk. The wheel wells were rusted clean through the fenders, the dash was rent with gaping cracks showing the sunbaked foam beneath, the padding in the seats had long since crumbled to dust. Everything about the car was thin and brittle, but somehow it still got Michel from A to B, and if he was to be believed he never had to do anything to it but give it a quart or two of oil every now and then when it happened to cross his mind.

A hollow metallic echo reverberated through Aoust's ears as he got in and shut the door. Michel started the car, and a loud, raspy growl sounded from the back and did not abate.

"That doesn't sound good," Aoust observed.

"The muffler fell off a couple months back on the 101. There was a big fuckin chunk of truck tire in the middle of the lane, which I couldn't see until the last minute because there was another truck in front of me, and I ran right over it. Ripped the muffler clean off. I saw it tumbling down the road in my rearview mirror, other cars swerving around it. Fuckin hilarious."

"So get a new muffler."

"It's on the list. I just haven't got around to it. The sound actually isn't that bad. It's the exhaust fumes that kick your ass, especially when you're stopped in traffic. It shouldn't be too bad once we're on the highway. I had to tape up the gearshift cover, the fumes were coming up through it."

Aoust looked where Michel was pointing and saw strips of red-white-and-blue US Postal Service packing tape wrapped around the gear stick and the skirting.

Michel pulled out and drove them south down Telegraph towards downtown Oakland, every rut and pot hole in the street jarring Aoust's tailbone. Michel steered with one hand, the other resting casually on the gear shift knob, exposing to Aoust's resigned eyes the cobra tattoo on his right forearm.

"Where are we going?" Aoust asked.

"Priceland."

Aoust looked at him. "Priceland? I thought we were going to a computer store?"

"They're cheaper there. I already did a search. Plus I need to pick up a few things."

"But Priceland?"

"You'll be fine."

Aoust wasn't sure about that.

At 58th Street Michel took the freeway exit, putting them onto the 980 through Oakland, then onto 880 South. It never took long for the anxiety to set in when Aoust ventured beyond the twenty-block diameter that constituted his primary sphere of activity. It was a hazy day, the sky glaring white. The vast gray sea of urban sprawl flowed around them, relegating the Berkeley Hills to minor brown incumbrances dwarfed by the towering signs of fast food franchises, gas stations, hotels, sports arenas. Aoust fought back each wave of existential nausea by reminding himself that at the end of this he would have the computer he needed to use the program to transcribe the tapes so he could write the book that would help him keep his job.

Even if they had been inclined to do so, the noise of the car as it labored to maintain sixty miles per hour would have made it nearly impossible for Aoust and Michel to speak and be heard. Aoust lit a cigarette and went to crack the window a few inches only to notice that the handle was missing. Seeing his father's predicament, Michel opened his own window. He grabbed his chrome-plated e-cig from the dash and took a few puffs himself. Aoust had tried Michel's e-cigarette, chuckled at the novelty of it, but he wasn't at all impressed with that sterile contraption, for long before this he had come to realize that the essential pleasure of smoking was precisely the presence of death hovering around the fringes, lurking in the smoke, for in that momentary if rarely conscious embrace of death there was a quickening of life itself, all the sweeter for its proximity to the grave. It was this vital dram of death that was entirely absent from the inert vapor issuing from the coils of these little electronic gizmos, a vapor born of the same utopian philosophy underlying the universal infatuation with computer technology, with "smart" phones, with drones to remotely kill your enemies with, with apps to wipe your ass for you—the illusion of getting something for nothing, when in fact you were just getting nothing.

Aoust smoked his cigarette and stared out the window, his general despair over humanity tempered somewhat by the raw physicality of the noise and speed.

Half an hour later, Michel exited the freeway on Dyer Street in Union City and turned into the Priceland parking lot. He coasted between the endless rows of parked cars for a while, but finding no free spots in the nearer territories, he settled for one a quarter of a mile from the entrance, back on the banks of the freeway, where a few forlorn ornamental pear trees struggled for life in the blazing heat of the asphalt. They got out and set off on their journey across the lot, steering clear of the variety of hazards that beset them along the way.

Aoust's relief when the refrigerated air struck his face was instantly dispelled by the impact of the rest of the store. He stopped just inside the door, bowled over by the vision before him. The only thing he could compare it to was the check-in area at Charles de Gaulle, the same inhuman magnitude, the same antlike swarms teeming through predetermined channels in a vast amphitheater of supply and demand, so monumental that it instantly filled him with a paralyzing anxiety. The aisles appeared to have no end, stretching so far into the distance that his eyes, even with the aid of what he had thought was a very good prescription, could not see to their end; they just softened to a faraway blur, like the avenues of Manhattan, only the light in here was not of a terrestrial wavelength but something cold and alien. The floor below it all gave off a blinding white sheen, creating the illusion that everyone was actually floating slightly above it, being pulled along by some irresistible force that likewise lulled them into a stupor of contentment, knowing as they did that nowhere else on Earth would they find a better price. To Aoust this was nothing less than a vision of hell—damned to roam the aisles of Priceland for all eternity, walled in on every side by cheap merchandise manufactured in China.

"I can't do this," he said.

Michel looked at him, and seeing the pallid terror on his face asked him what was wrong.

"Please, let's go back. I don't need a new computer."

"For fuck's sake, Dad. It's just a store. We'll only be here half an hour. If you don't want to get the computer here, fine, but let's at least take a look at them now that we're here. Besides, I told you I need to pick up a few other things. Come on."

And so Aoust, not wanting to look like a coward in his son's eyes, allowed himself to be talked into looking at the computers, determined though he now was not to buy anything here, just look at them, let the salesman give his pitch, then, if Michel could convince him one more time of the efficacy of the transcription program, then maybe he would go and buy the machine somewhere else, from some little shop in Berkeley on the verge of bankruptcy, where he would happily pay whatever the poor fellow asked, relishing into the bargain the knowledge of how much he had lost by not procuring it from the voracious maw of megacapitalism.

Locating the shopping carts, Michel yanked one out of the train and set it in motion before them. Soon they were gliding along between canyon walls of merchandise like Gulliver in the land of Brobdingnag, everything seemingly made for giants. In time they entered into an area itself bigger than a normal-sized store, row upon row of open laptops locked down with wire cables, flanked by walls of monitors and giant flat panel TVs all playing the same cataclysmic superhero movie at deafening volumes, the floor quaking with every explosion, cars hurtling through the air on every screen, disgustingly muscled bodies defying the laws of physics, everything screaming out in supersaturated high-definition color.

Arriving at a rank of glass counters behind which several young employees in red shirts and black pants were staring into space with bovine expressions, Michel asked after a certain computer, and the worker, a mere girl, returned to consciousness and came around the counter and escorted them over to the aisles of laptops and pointed out the model Michel had asked about and rattled off a stream of gibberish, acronyms, numbers, strange technobabble which to Aoust's ears may as well have been the language spoken on some other planet. The girl disappeared, and

Michel fiddled around with the machine for a while, which according to the plastic information strip behind it cost $569.00, telling his father that this was the best price he would find, and he too poured forth a torrent of gibberish in that same alien language, but with all the thumping and crashing going on around him Aoust couldn't understand anything Michel was saying.

"What?" he shouted to Michel's unintelligible question.

"I said do you want to get it?"

"Yes! Just get the fucking thing and let's get the hell out of here. I'm going insane."

So Michel extracted one of the boxes from the shelves below and set it in the main cavity of the enormous three-tiered cart and led them away from the battle zone. Once they could converse again at a normal volume, Michel said he needed to pick up some packs of razors. He pushed the cart, and Aoust followed at his side as they ventured forth into still more distant realms, strange domains of ketchup bottles the size of televisions; entire campgrounds set up on artificial grass with walk-in tents and barbecue grills and lounge chairs; an armory of high-power rifles and ammunition. Every now and then an obese man or woman would glide through the nearest intersection on a little electric vehicle with its own dedicated cart in front. In time Michel found his razors and tossed bags of them into the cart. While they were here, he said, he might as well pick up some other things that were cheaper here than in the city: a 25-pound box of laundry detergent, 72 rolls of toilet paper, a box of 100 jumbo size garbage bags.

The cart laboring under the load, they made their way up to the check-out aisles, which again reminded Aoust of an airport, only now it was the arrivals hall with its countless immigration control kiosks with every shade of humanity lined up to prove their legitimacy and be granted entrance to the promised land. They joined the shortest line they could find, which nonetheless tailed out into the thoroughfare, and there they waited with their fellow shoppers, slowly progressing, inch by inch, as those before them emptied their mountains of merchandise onto the conveyor belt and perused the shelves of gums and lip balms and batteries and candies as they impatiently waited for it all to be scanned and bagged and deposited back into their carts.

When it was time to pay, Aoust pulled out his credit card and didn't have much trouble convincing Michel to let him pay for his stuff too. At last they were free, out again in the scorching heat, navigating their cart around parking and backing-out cars on the return journey to the far end of the parking lot, where they loaded the stuff into the back of the Beast, got in, and set off once more for Berkeley.

The air didn't cool down again until they reached the border of Oakland.

"Are you hungry?" Aoust asked as Michel came off the freeway onto Telegraph Avenue.

"I'm all right."

"Let's go get something to eat."

"It's not even five yet."

"So what? Let's go to Orchid. You still like

Thai, right?"

"Sure."

Michel drove them down to Shattuck Avenue.

"Rajdani Palace?" he said in bafflement as he pulled to a stop in front of what used to be Orchid.

"Are you sure this is the right block?" Aoust asked.

"Of course. There's Radio Shack. It's gone under. I wonder when that happened? That sucks, man."

They sat there for a while, staring through the windshield at the unfamiliar sign.

"What do you want to do?" Michel asked. "Should we try this place?"

"No. Maybe we should just forget it. You're not hungry anyway."

"I am now. Come on. How about Plearn? I'm sure they're still open."

Aoust made no protest, but he wasn't thrilled about the prospect of going to Plearn. He'd had his heart set on Orchid. Although he couldn't remember the last time they had eaten there, his memory was still filled with all the times they had done so as a family during Michel's childhood: images of Michel in a wooden booster seat, Helen teaching him how to use chopsticks, Michel on various birthdays, Michel with his high school girlfriend. Aoust would readily admit that it was never the greatest cuisine on the planet, but for whatever reason it had been one of their mainstays, where the family tensions always melted away as soon as they stepped through the door.

Michel managed to find a parking spot on University Avenue, a few blocks down from the restaurant, and luckily Aoust had some quarters in his pockets. Aoust lit a cigarette and Michel puffed on his e-cig as they walked up the south side of the street. Crossing Milvia, Aoust was pained to see the scruffy old UC Theater marquee with a realtor's placard on it—the title of this tragic story: "AVAILABLE," with a phone number beneath it. In an even more depressing irony, the sealed-up front of the building was papered over with posters for current Hollywood releases, one of which was called *Doomsday*.

"Look at this shit," Aoust said to Michel as they passed under the marquee. "Did I ever tell you that I saw in 1978 Werner Herzog eat his own shoe in there, right there on the stage?"

"Yes, Dad."

"He lost a bet to Errol Morris that he'd never finish *Gates of Heaven*. Funniest thing I ever saw. Better than Chaplin."

"I first saw *The Rocky Horror Picture Show* there."

"Yes. Your mother and I saw it there too."

"Me and Chris snuck out one night when he was spending the night, rode our bikes down here, smoked some pot, watched the film."

"Was that in high school?"

"No, junior high."

Aoust chuckled.

"They're supposedly trying to turn it into a music venue," Michel said.

"Better than a billboard for Hollywood."

"Who knows, maybe we'll play there someday."

Aoust nodded.

In the restaurant they were shown to a table and given the menus, and after they ordered, Aoust told Michel that he'd enjoyed the show, recounting in amusing Aoustian fashion the troubles he'd had getting home (wrong bus, etc.). He asked Michel how things were going at his job, not knowing until then that Michel had quit the job in question last month and was now working at a Russian Hill restaurant, days only, leaving him more time for the band. Aoust asked after Michel's girlfriend, he couldn't remember her name, not knowing that Michel had changed girlfriends as well, which got a chuckle from them both. The new one's name was Maya, and she was the same age as he was, Michel said, intimating that this was progress. All in all it was a pleasant dinner, an acceptable substitute for Orchid after all, the food actually better, the restaurant nearly empty at that time of day and therefore blessedly quiet, Aoust in particular feeling a sense of accomplishment for having survived the Priceland ordeal despite his moments of weakness. Michel too was in an expansive and generous mood, asking his father about his writing and his troubles in the department, seeming genuinely interested to know the answers.

Back in Aoust's apartment, Michel got to work setting up the laptop, personalizing it for his father, getting rid of all the stuff he knew Aoust wouldn't need, downloading other things he knew he would. From his own memory stick he downloaded the audio enhancement software. Finally, he asked for his father's credit card details so he could download the French version of the transcription software.

While the audio enhancement software was capturing the Defoix tape, Michel began giving his father, and himself, a tutorial on the transcription software. As Michel spoke of training the system to recognize the speech patterns of each speaker, of creating user profiles, of deep learning, of pull-down menus and acoustic models and hot keys, Aoust realized that it was hopeless. He would never be able to figure it all out. There was no choice but to carry on as before, as painful and maddening as it was. For two hours, as Michel futilely labored to try to get the program to accurately transcribe even a single sentence of the Defoix tape, the most noise-free tape of the lot, Aoust kept these thoughts to himself.

"Listen, Michel," he said, growing weary of staring at the screen and watching the computer spit out every variant of the phonemes but the correct one, "it's not working. Let's call it a night."

"It'll work," Michel insisted. "You just have to train it."

"I can't sit here wasting my time training this machine to do what I can already do myself."

"Then why the hell did you shell out all this money?"

"I thought it would be easier, but clearly it isn't."

Michel kept trying.

"Come, Michel. Enough. You've done all you can."

At last Michel relented, saying that he could come back tomorrow if Aoust wanted him to, all of these valiant efforts, Aoust knew, merely a prelude to Michel asking for another loan, so that it was something of a relief when he finally did, with the usual mix of feigned humility and genuine irritation, on his way to the door.

"How much do you need?" Aoust asked.

"Five hundred would be nice."

Aoust told him he would do the transfer first thing in the morning.

They hugged at the door.

After Michel had gone, Aoust closed the new laptop, wrapped up the cables, shoved it back into its box and tucked it away on the high shelf of his bedroom closet.

•

Fearing that he was losing the battle with the glorious spring day pouring through the classroom windows, Aoust launched into a personal anecdote.

"Forty years ago tomorrow, on May 2nd, 1968, I was privileged to be on hand when Henri Langlois, by then officially reinstated as the director of the Cinémathèque Française, reopened the Left Bank screening room. That very day the administrators at Nanterre, where I was a student, shut down the university, unable to quell the relentless provocations. The next day we stormed the Sorbonne. I was there in the Latin Quarter with thousands of other students, lighting fires in the roads, melting the tar to get at the stones beneath. The first paving stone of May '68 flew at a police van that night, shattering its windshield. No, it wasn't me," he added with a small smile.

"Now some might argue that aesthetics plays at best only a minor role in the theater of politics," Aoust forged on, resorting once more to his lecture notes, "but I would argue that art, especially cinema, was a crucial conduit for the revolutionary message of the students of May '68. Even the most cynical historians don't deny that the student uprisings were the spark that set all of France ablaze with revolutionary zeal. It is a testament to the power of cinema that a film like Michel Defoix's *Le Retour*, a forgotten masterpiece of the silent era, which unfortunately I can't show you because it no longer exists, can reach across the abyss of time, if only through our collective unconscious, and—"

"Uh, excuse me, Professor Aoust," the anarchist student interrupted. "It's actually on YouTube."

"That's the Gaumont documentary, not the actual film," Aoust replied and carried on with the lecture.

A few minutes later the anarchist student raised his phone.

"*Le Retour*, 1923. Directed by Michel Defoix."

Aoust, if only to humor the kid and his toy, walked over to him and took a look at the screen of the phone, on which the cow slaughter scene was presently playing. Aoust had never watched it on anything smaller than a television, which was bad enough, but to see the cow reduced to two inches on a cell phone, surrounded by icons for other videos, instantly depressed him. The anarchist handed him the phone, and Aoust watched another ten seconds or so, waiting for the segue to *Ménilmontant* and the narrator's discussion of the cine clubs. But to his surprise the scene kept going, into the farmhouse dinner scene. So it wasn't the Gaumont documentary after all. Someone must have digitized the Cinémathèque Française elements, or uploaded one of the rare video copies.

Aoust stood beside the anarchist's chair, looking down at the screen in his palm, amazed at the clarity of the images, which he hadn't thought possible on a cell phone, waiting to experience the disappointment anew in yet another ephemeral medium. If there was any gratification at all in seeing *Le Retour* on a cell phone it was only in knowing that no matter how many gadgets mankind invented, all things sooner or later must perish, and despite the feelings of personal affront that he began to feel as it sank in that the film was now in the public domain, he lost himself as always in the movement of Michel as he got up from the dining table and walked towards the door, a door he would never reach. Only this time he did reach the door. He raised his right hand and opened it. He stepped out into a moonlit night. He walked across the farmyard to the barn. He went into the barn and led the cow out.

A sharp electric shock jolted Aoust's internal organs, radiating instantly to his extremities. He stood stock still, staring down in disbelief at the tiny screen in the palm of his hand, wherein Michel was now entering the village the next morning to sell the cow, a scene Aoust had imagined a thousand times but never seen with his own eyes. His mind raced to explain where the missing scenes had come from, but the film was unfolding faster than his thoughts, revealing yet another frame every sixteenth of a second that he had never seen before.

"This can't be."

He nervously asked the student to rewind it back to the beginning, and with the phone again in his hand Aoust saw two young boys enter a carnival tent and make their way to the front and sit in the dirt to gaze up in rapture at the scenes of Parisian life blazing across the movie screen before them. Aoust watched, uncomprehending, mouth agape, his pounding heart making it difficult to breathe. He felt his limbs go weak, his bowels soften, something he hadn't felt since the day Helen announced she wanted a divorce. He stood this way for several minutes, staring down in shock at the screen, then he handed the phone back to the student and returned in a daze to the table at the front of the class.

By this point the rest of the students were either looking down at their own cell phones or staring at Aoust with barely concealed annoyance. He felt dizzy. He made a feeble effort to continue where he had left off, but he couldn't concentrate. He struggled valiantly on for a few more minutes then apologized and dismissed the class, saying he wasn't feeling well. On his way out, the anarchist student asked him if there was anything he could do for him, but Aoust brushed him off, saying it was only low blood sugar.

He remained seated at the table long after the students had gone. Eventually he pulled himself together enough to gather up his papers and put them in his case and shuffle out of the classroom.

He had to talk to someone. He walked in a daze to the elevator and joined the throng of students piling into it and pressed the button for the sixth floor. "Hold the 'vator!" someone shouted, and the doors jerked open at the last second to squeeze another body in. Oblivious of Aoust's impatience, the elevator ascended with its customary languor. When at last the doors parted and, apologizing, he nudged the bodies obstructing him, Aoust got out and made his way along the corridor only to realize when he reached a solid wall where the steps down into the north wing should have been that he wasn't on the right level to cross; he had to go down another level, and too impatient to wait for the elevator to make its leisurely rounds, he backtracked to the stairwell and took it down, and this time he successfully crossed over into the north wing, made his way to the other stairwell, back up to the sixth floor and along the corridor to his colleague Elias Kiss's office. Only it wasn't Kiss's office. The plaque on the door read "Walter Schacke." It soon became apparent, from the plaques on the other doors and the posters and flyers and cartoons on the corkboards, that this was German territory, and for a few surreal seconds Aoust wondered what had become of the Film department, until, realizing his mistake, he went back to the stairwell and up again to the real sixth floor, where he did in fact find Kiss's office still there, if not Kiss himself.

Aoust didn't want to see anyone else in the department, so he carried on down the corridor to his own office, thinking there was still a chance it wasn't real, that it was some kind of elaborate recreation, done with computer graphics. He needed to sit down and watch it again, on a bigger screen; he needed a computer with internet.

In his office he tore all the Post-its off the monitor and turned on the computer. He could hear the Geiger-counter clicking of the hard drive straining to do something, but nothing appeared on the screen for well over two minutes. Finally various icons began to emerge and, at last, the university logo. But when he went to open the browser he was informed that the version of the browser he was using was no longer supported and it was recommended that he update it to the new one at the provided link, which he subsequently pressed. He was taken to another page, with another link, which he also clicked. He kept pressing the buttons he was told to press until the new browser was downloaded, and after five minutes of various notifications and advice and promotions and tutorials, he was informed that the browser he was using was incompatible with his current operating system. He cursed the machine and turned it off.

Not one of the thousands of students milling about in the warm spring sunshine of the Berkeley campus was aware of the epic drama unfolding in the heart and mind of Professor Aoust as he made his way hurriedly across Sproul Plaza, over to Telegraph Avenue, through the hawkers and homeless, back to his apartment. He immediately checked his answering machine to see if by chance anyone had called to inform him of the news, but the red light was calm and steady, calmer and steadier than him, which raised his hopes that it really was a hoax.

He went to his desk, on which all the tapes and the rest of his materials for the book were scattered around, and turned on his old desktop computer, opened the browser, and typed in "Le Retour Utube," which Google correctly interpreted for him. Proceeding to YouTube he clicked on the big play button, but the screen remained black while some translucent dots began a clockwise revolution. Nearly a minute later an ad for a hair cream commenced playing, with the option of skipping it in five seconds. The screen froze for a while on a balding pate. In time the countdown commenced, and Aoust seized his chance to skip the rest of the ad. At last the carnival scene started and played for about five seconds before freezing. Aoust waited. He pressed the play button repeatedly while cursing the machine, with no result. He tried to close the browser, but it too was frozen now.

Aoust stood up from the desk and lit a desperately needed cigarette. As the nicotine entered his bloodstream and began to soothe his nerves, he was able to think more clearly. He hurried to his bedroom closet, pulled the new laptop out of the box, carried it over to the sofa and turned it on. Soon he was watching the opening scene again, the boys in the carnival tent watching the film, and again he could not believe what he was seeing. Here, eighty-five years after its disappearance, was the magical little scene that Nadine Fernex had so vividly described in her recollections of the film, the scene Defoix himself had reminisced about on that sweltering August day in 1972. But it wasn't magic that Aoust was feeling. It was shock.

Scene after scene, it soon became perfectly clear to Aoust that this was not some computer-generated fabrication: those really were the streets of Paris in 1923; this really was Nadia Marinescu and Michel Defoix; these really were the storied scratches Defoix had made on the negative with a dental instrument; it was all there, exactly as Aoust had imagined it, yet somehow not as he had imagined it at all. Perhaps more disconcerting than the restored scenes were the ones he had watched countless times before, if only because all the imperfections that his brain had become so accustomed to over the past four decades were now gone: the unintentional scratches, the dust and hairs, the mangled and missing frames, the washed-out tone—all of it was gone. This was a new print, apparently in immaculate condition. And while he could not deny that his eyes were enraptured by what they were seeing, he knew it was nothing more than the instinctual thrill one experiences in the face of a natural disaster, the same strange and terrible elation a man must feel when the wave of a tsunami looms up out of the suddenly silent sea before wiping him off the face of the planet.

He watched the film to the end, then sat there for a long time, staring blankly at the screen. Recommended to him in the column on the right were such fare as "Indian Baby Toss Ritual," "Drunk History," "*Star Wars* According to a Three-Year-Old," "Tom Cruise Scientology Video," "'Yes We Can' by will.i.am," and more.

It wasn't until he was about to fold down the screen that it suddenly struck him. Where was the sex scene? He hit the play button again and dragged the time bar back and forth through the entire film, scanning the still frames for nude flesh, but there was none to be seen. No hint at all of even the tamest courtship ritual between Michel and Nadia. Only then did he notice the running time: 26 minutes. According to every reliable historical record, the length of the film that was screened on Friday, November 23, 1923, was thirty-two minutes.

He clicked to Google and typed in various combinations of "Le Retour," "film," "Michel Defoix," "discovered," and "new print," first in English, then in French, until at last, on the fourth page of suggested links he found it in last month's events calendar of the Cinémathèque Française webpage. A tiny window for Friday, February 15, 2008, 6:30 pm, stating nothing more than the title, the director, a brief synopsis, and the production details. The only thing indicating that this wasn't a screening of the scraps from the vault was the running time: 26 min. He combed the rest of the website for anything whatsoever relating to the screening of the new print but found nothing.

Extraordinary circumstances call for extraordinary actions. Aoust decided it was time he broke his e-mail silence and contacted his colleagues around the world to try to get some answers. When he went to open his university e-mail account it asked him for his password. He typed in what he thought it should be, but a message in red informed him that the password was incorrect. He typed it again, thinking maybe he had mistyped it. Again it was incorrect. He tried a variant he thought he remembered having used at one time, and this time after he typed it he was informed that he was locked out of his account.

He picked up the phone and called the Pacific Film Archive and asked to speak with Marsha.

"Do you know about Le Retour?" he said when she came on the line.

"The new print? Yes. Isn't it wonderful news?"

"So you do know?"

"Yes. Didn't you know?"

"How long have you known?"

"Oh, I guess a few weeks. Susan Cathala at the Cinémathèque told me."

"No one told me."

"I assumed you knew."

"No. I only just found out. It's on YouTube."

"Isn't it wonderful?"

Aoust made no reply.

"It's a shame we didn't know sooner," Marsha said. "We could've included it in the silent program."

"What do you know about it?"

"Only that the son had it all these years."

"Who's son?"

"Defoix's, I assume."

"Defoix had no son. He had no children at

all."

"That's all she said, the son."

"Very strange. What else did she say?"

"We didn't talk much about it. I was calling her about something else."

"Can I get Susan's number from you?"

"Hold on a second."

She gave him the number.

After hanging up, Aoust checked his watch. A little after five. Two o'clock in the morning Paris time. He would have to wait until midnight to try calling the Cinémathèque. In the meantime he did more Google searches, but apart from the Cinémathèque screening, it was all old stuff.

He watched the film again. He smoked several packs of cigarettes. He thought about calling a few other film scholars he occasionally communicated with on the East Coast, but the only phone numbers he could find for them were office numbers, and he knew they wouldn't be in. He considered calling his sister, but he didn't want to panic her in the middle of the night, and he knew she wouldn't understand anyway. He tried to read but couldn't concentrate. He started and abandoned three different films. He went out for a walk, and it seemed that everything he saw and heard was cut off from him behind a thick wall of glass. He bought some cigarettes and returned home.

He waited until ten after midnight then dialed the number Marsha had given him. Susan answered, and they had the following conversation in French.

"This is Bernard Aoust, from Berkeley."

"Oh, good morning Professor Aoust. Nice to hear from you. Are you here in Paris?"

"No, Berkeley."

"You're calling from Berkeley? Isn't it the middle of the night there?"

"Just after midnight."

"Well, I feel honored. How can I help you?"

"I've just found out about the new print of Michel Defoix's *Le Retour*."

"Did you not get my e-mails?"

"No. I didn't."

"Check your spam. I wondered why I didn't get any replies from you, but I figured you must be busy. We had a screening last month. I'd been hoping you could attend."

"I wish you'd called."

"You know, the time difference. I figured e-mail was the better option."

"I just saw it on YouTube."

"Ugh. Don't remind me. I've already filed a complaint."

"So it's real? This is a genuine print?"

"Better. It's a dupe negative. Pristine condition. There's only one break in the entire 1691 feet of film."

"A splice?"

"No. The film was in two pieces."

"Do you have a few minutes?"

She did, and so Aoust started in with his questions, and she told him what she knew. She said that in early January the Cinémathèque had been approached by a man named Léopold Viette, offering to sell them a film. He had purchased it as part of a lot of the estate of someone named Michel

Gomot, who had died in Rouen in September of 2006. This man, Viette, who made a living by reselling his estate sale finds on eBay and other sites, had no particular interest in cinema and so had done nothing about the film for over a year until a fellow estate sale scavenger convinced him it might be worth something. Viette did a little research, which eventually led him to Susan at the Cinémathèque, where of course they were all amazed and delighted to be offered the film once they realized what it was (she didn't disclose how much they had paid for it). Among the personal effects of the lot that Viette had purchased was a typed, three-page autobiography of Michel Gomot, written a year before his death, which Viette gave to the Cinémathèque when they purchased the film, and from which Susan was able to glean some of the salient details of Michel Gomot's life, probably the most incredible being that he was the biological son of Nadia Marinescu. Born Michel Marinescu on May 15, 1924, in Argenteuil, on the outskirts of Paris, to Nadia Marinescu and an unnamed father, he was given up to the state at birth and adopted in July of 1924 by Fernand and Édith Gomot, a couple in their early forties who had lost their only son in the First World War. When Nadia Marinescu died in 1929, she willed her few possessions to her son, among which was this duplicate negative of *Le Retour*. As he was only five years old at the time of her death, it was left to the Gomots to bequeath the film to their adopted son at the appropriate time. When Michel was seven, the Gomots moved from Saint-Denis to Mouthe, a tiny village in the

Jura Mountains on the Swiss border. Fernand Gomot was a Huguenot pastor, and he and his wife remained living in the village until their deaths in 1965 and 1967 respectively. Michel Gomot reveals in the autobiographical sketch that while he knew from an early age who his real mother was, and that he eventually managed to see some of the films she had acted in, he never knew about *Le Retour* and didn't find out about the existence of the print she had willed to him until after the deaths of his adoptive parents. After Édith Gomot's death he found the film in a single canister inside a locked trunk in the basement of the family home in Mouthe. Susan told Aoust that the year-round freezing temperatures of a basement at that altitude must have preserved the film from decay. She and her fellow archivists had determined that the duplicate negative was made from the original interpositive, and she also told Aoust that there was an original label on the canister from Rapid Films, Bernard Natan's lab. In the rest of his brief autobiography Michel Gomot speaks mostly about his life as a chemical engineer, his travels, and his choice not to marry or have children.

"He says nothing else about the film?" Aoust asked Susan, exasperated by the lack of information. "Why he never tried to do something with it?"

"He doesn't say anything else about the film."

"What about the sex scene?"

"It's not there. That's where the film was cut. Everything between 989 and 1367 feet was missing. We were really upset about that. I called Léopold Viette and spoke to him again, asking if he had seen any other pieces of film, either in his lot or in the rest of the estate sale, and he said he hadn't."

"He could have cut it himself."

"I don't think so. I got the impression that he hadn't looked beyond the first few frames. I even called the auction house and spoke with their appraiser, and she insisted that there were no other pieces of film in the estate."

"Maybe this Michel Gomot himself cut it. It could be why he kept it to himself."

"We'll probably never know, since there's no way of determining when the cut was made. We don't even know how Nadia came to be in possession of the dupe, or even who made it. Obviously the dupe was made sometime before she died, so there's about a four-year window there. It's conceivable that Bernard Natan made the dupe for protection, and somehow she got it through him. But any number of people could have cut the sex scene, including Nadia herself. She was clearly proud enough of the film to will it to her son, but it's understandable if she didn't want him to see her like that. Or was it Fernand or Édith Gomot, a well-intentioned attempt to spare their adopted son the shame of his mother's past? We just don't know."

Aoust asked a few more questions, and she answered them as well as she could, but he sensed her getting antsy to get back to work, so he thanked her for her time and said he should let her go.

He sat smoking for another half hour or so, thinking. If Susan's information, and his own calculations were correct, Michel Gomot must have been conceived in August or September of 1923, the very months when Defoix was shooting *Le Retour*. Was it possible that the only child of Michel Defoix and Nadia Marinescu was conceived during the very act of coitus that in the end destroyed them both?

Aoust stubbed out his last cigarette and went to bed, but he could not sleep.

•

The spring semester drew to a close. Aoust went to his classes and delivered his lectures and sat through his silent office hours. He showed his film clips and graded student essays. He attended screenings at the PFA. He spoke with his sister every Sunday morning on the phone. He fed Musidora and smoked cigarettes and went for solitary walks at night. The days grew warmer and longer. The London plane trees on Sproul Plaza came into leaf. The rhododendrons and magnolias flowered in the glades.

One evening in late May, on his way home from his office, Aoust saw the computer smashers again on Lower Sproul Plaza, with the usual bemused bystanders dotting the fringes while the pounders pranced around the shifting pile like Hollywood Indians around a bonfire. Aoust watched them with detachment, moved almost to pity by the futility of such gestures. As he continued on past the ruckus, one of the smashers, a young guy with a scraggly beard and round mirrored sunglasses, turned and caught sight of Aoust and, holding out a blue aluminum baseball bat, said, "Here, Pops. Kill this shit." Aoust hesitated, sure that the man was just trying to get a laugh from the crowd at his expense, but there was a certain stony insistence in the young man's voice which conveyed that he was in earnest.

Aoust grabbed the bat. He scanned the pile for something not yet obliterated, and spying an intact old monitor with a convex screen, he drew nearer and took position. Gripping the handle of the bat with both hands, he raised it high above his head and swung down with all his might on the dull, dark screen. Upon impact the glass imploded with a satisfying concussion. Aoust raised the bat again. Again and again he pounded the monitor, pulverizing every shard of glass, breaking the plastic housing into a dozen pieces, pummeling the inner circuitry to an unrecognizable lump of metal. His heart racing now, he located another unscathed peripheral and unleashed on it. A cheer went up from the crowd.

All around the pile the old man went, pounding everything that wasn't yet shattered, cursing every piece he struck with all that remained of his breath.

About the Author

James Terry is the author of a short story collection, *Kingdom of the Sun* (University of New Mexico Press, 2016), and two novels, *The Solitary Woman of Shakespeare Sandstone* (Skyhorse, 2016) and *Heir Apparent* (Skyhorse, 2019). His short stories have been nominated multiple times for the Pushcart and O.Henry prizes.